African/American Library

General Editor *Charles R. Larson*

A continuing series of works of literary excellence by black writers in the United States, Africa and the Caribbean.

THE LOOMING SHADOW

by Legson Kayira

With an Introduction by Harold R. Collins

COLLIER BOOKS

The Macmillan Company
866 Third Avenue, New York, N.Y. 10022
Collier-Macmillan Canada Ltd., Toronto, Ontario

First Collier Books Edition 1970

The Looming Shadow was first published in a hardcover edition by Doubleday & Company, Inc., and is reprinted by arrangement.

Library of Congress Catalog Card Number: 76-117962

Printed in the United States of America

To Pegy Lane

INTRODUCTION

Legson Kayira is a remarkable young man whose life has often seemed incredible. Born in the village of Mpale in the Karonga District of the Nyasaland Protectorate, now Malawi, in the late thirties or early forties (Kayira doesn't know exactly which year), he came very close to being an infant mortality. His immature mother, fatigued with carrying such a big, fat baby around on her back, simply dumped him into the Didimu River. Luckily he was fished out by a scandalized neighbor. Kayira's family was very poor, so poor that the village headman—who was perhaps as wise as Mwenimuzi of *The Looming Shadow*—saw fit to report to the tax collector that Kayira's father was dead, to save him from paying the poll tax. In spite of the family's extreme poverty, Legson went to various primary schools and, though he was hard-pressed to dress himself decently, to the distinguished Livingstonia Secondary School.

His schooling must have given him a perhaps excessive admiration for things English, for his Christian name is one he made up, to sound English, possibly suggested by his older brother's name, Tennyson. He decided that he wanted to continue his education in America, "the land of Lincoln," which his poor unsophisticated mother thought was a mere five days' walk away from their home. To say that this young African was determined to have an American education is an understatement. What he proposed, incredible as it may seem, was to *walk* from his home to Alexandria or Port Said and work his way on a freighter to New York. He started out with a bag containing five days' supply of flour, an extra khaki shirt, an English Bible, a copy of *Pilgrim's Progress*, and an axe. He was wearing his school uniform shirt with a badge bearing its Browningesque motto: *I Will Try*. And he did in fact walk from his Malawi village into Tanzania, through Tanzania and Uganda and the Sudan, to Khartoum. He got several bicycle rides in Tanzania; he hitched some rides on trucks in Uganda and the Sudan; and went across Lake Victoria and down the Nile in steamers; but it was mostly walking—certainly one of the heroic athletic feats of our rather unheroic century. Along the long way he supported himself by doing odd jobs and slept in country villages, rest houses, and the homes of new-made friends and well-wishers. He pretty much lived on bananas.

When he started out on this journey he had no notion whatsoever of where he would go to school in America. But in a U.S. Information Service library in Kampala he chanced upon a directory of American junior colleges and opened it at random on the name of Skagit Valley Junior College, Mount Vernon, Washington; he sent off a request for a scholarship, which was readily awarded to him. After some difficulty getting a transit visa for the Sudan, he finally got to Khartoum, where he was held up by the American embassy officials because he could not meet the financial requirements for an American visa. However, being notified of the difficulty, the Skagit Valley College faculty and students and the local community rose to the occasion splendidly, set up a Legson Kayira Fund, and brought him to America in fine style.

At Skagit Valley Legson made the students snigger a bit when he solemnly announced to them that he "hoped someday to be president, prime minister or something of that order" in his own country, for young Americans no longer believe that each one of them has a chance of becoming President and they usually lack the intense dedication of young Africans. As we might expect, Legson was a good student: he read far more than other students, taking out of the college library books on subjects ranging from nuclear physics to John Locke. He was "fiercely independent" in doing his college assignments, dodging those which would not be useful to him "in parliament." His thirty-year time-table for himself would be ridiculously grandiose for anyone besides a young man who had walked the length of Africa for an American education: "1960–70: Education in the United States, with master's and doctor's degree in both physical and political science; 1970–90: Teaching in Nyasaland, government service, and perhaps, marriage."

The reader who enjoys *The Looming Shadow* should read Kayira's autobiography, *I Will Try,* one of the best of the African autobiographies, which brings his story up to his entrance into the University of Washington. Readers of the autobiography will notice that Kayira knew well two witch doctors who may have been models for Simbwindimbwi in *The Looming Shadow:* his family "doctor," who was consulted when his father feared he was being bewitched and who was a frequent visitor at their house; and his maternal grandfather, who was a celebrated practitioner and who took young Legson on his herb-hunting expeditions. In the autobiography we also learn that Legson Kayira had good cause to know a great deal about the traditional African belief in witchcraft. His own father was a strong believer in witchcraft and it was a "popular practice at the time, and still is, though not so pronounced as before."

The autobiography throws some light on Legson's antecedents as a writer. It is surely significant that the two books he carried with him on his great African walk were the Bible and Bunyan's *Pilgrim's Progress;* he refers frequently to the latter classic, secularizing the book somewhat in his use of it for inspiration, apparently equating an American education with the Celestial City itself. The autobiography mentions a great many speaking engagements at service clubs and church groups in the Skagit Valley area and farther afield; and interviews for magazines, newspapers, radio, and T.V.; such experience may well have made him more fluent in English and more articulate, and perhaps stirred his memory of African manners, African headmen, and witch doctors. In *I Will Try* Kayira explains how that work grew out of a short autobiographical sketch written for organizations he could not speak to, later developed into a paper for a University of Washington English professor.

Kayira has written a second novel, *Jingala,* which deals with an elderly hero of considerable intelligence. Jingala suffers two cruel disappointments: his son, in some ways an immature young man, scorns the life of the village, and decides to become a priest, thus rejecting many traditional beliefs; his young bride runs off to South Africa with a young mine worker, and is bound to be unhappy. Jingala is a man with a good deal of individuality, like the headman and the doctor in *The Looming Shadow*. In *Jingala,* as in *The Looming Shadow,* Kayira paints a pessimistic picture of Africa's future.

The Looming Shadow of the title of this novel is the "looming shadow of darkness left from antiquity, a reminder of their [the villagers'] past and dictator of their present." This darkness is probably equivalent to the "occasional fallacy" of tradition the author mentions, which the old men of the village, "tempered by tradition," are "weak to challenge." This darkness has its symbol in the eclipse of the sun at the opening of the story, which presages the death of a chief or other great man. It is significant that the novel begins with an eclipse, or more importantly, with the Kavukuku villagers' superstitious attitude toward the eclipse, and their chief's attempt to lock up the passerby who had reported a white man's confident prediction of the event. It is significant also that the first chapter gives an account of the present situation of witchcraft in the village, together with a hint that Musyani has the traditional appearance of a witch. We know right away that the darkness of superstition will be important in the novel, that the particular form the superstition will take will be belief in witchcraft, and that the victim of the fear and hostility aroused by this belief will be Musyani, who is not so much the central character of the novel as the character occasioning the central situation.

Musyani is charged with witchcraft, and this charge is in the very center of the action. We sympathize with his distress at being thus falsely charged, especially since he seems a decent, reasonably peaceful man who we know—by looking into his mind—to be innocent. And yet Yotamu Mwenimuzi, the village headman, is the real hero of the novel. He is responsible for good order in his community, for peace and harmony; he must dampen hostility like that between Matenda and Musyani, whose murderously bitter quarrel has sprung up over a woman. And the circumstances in which Mwenimuzi must work to bring about social harmony are extremely ticklish.

Mwenimuzi must adapt the traditional methods of social control to modern westernized conditions where the young men wear neatly-pressed khaki shorts and say "so what?" The poison ordeal for accused witches, used as a control device before the advent of the whites, is of course not allowed by the white authorities. And yet the villagers still believe in witchcraft and still feel disposed to accuse their enemies of practicing it; hence Mwenimuzi's toleration of Simbwindimbwi, the "doctor"; his symbolical adaptation of the traditional ordeal at the villagers' public meeting; and his attempt to make the dying Matenda's brother and son "cool it" and to punish them for arson and attempted murder after the burning of Musyani's house. But the white authorities at the Boma, or district headquarters, are as heavy-handed and as brutally imperceptive as the pioneer empire-builders who kidnapped Mwenimuzi's father and his father's men to help them capture the doughty slaver Mlozi. The white police officer who judges Mwenimuzi can understand only that Mwenimuzi has allowed a dangerous man like Simbwindimbwi to remain in the village, has taken no action against Matenda's brother, who had threatened Musyani, and has kept the poison *mwavi* in his house.

Kayira's handling of the character Mwenimuzi gives us a kind of detached admiration for him. We hardly ever look into his mind, as we do into Musyani's and Simbwindimbwi's; authorial commentary does not urge us to think well of him, nor are there any kinds of special devices to make him look good to us. There is merely a matter-of-fact and occasionally comic account of an intelligent leader of traditional orientatation trying to cope with an extremely difficult situation in a westernizing African village; he is an intelligent traditionalist caught between the passions of superstitious villagers and the ignorant harshness of alien overlords. We look over the doctor's shoulder at his crucial interview with the headman and note with him Mwenimuzi's "profound mood," "a mood almost verging on resignation," and his "compressed and resolute mouth," while he "continued to stare at the wall and seemed to be carried away by some secret thoughts."

It may seem incredible to the reader that an African headman who wears a butterfly-colored robe and automobile-tire sandals, who impresses laborers to build his house, and who can scarcely make the characters of the English alphabet, could have assimilated some of the fundamentals of European justice and be a fairminded and intelligent ruler of his little domain. Yet years ago the brilliant British anthropologist Audrey Richards observed that the Africans' assimilation of Western culture moves in strange and mysterious ways. She noted that a chief who dispenses justice from a "mud and wattle veranda" may have approached the mental attitude of the white man much more closely than the chief who has a brand new brick courthouse. Appearances are deceiving in Africa—as elsewhere. In externals Mwenimuzi may seem a bit uncouth, but he has an acute mind. He demands western-style evidence, not deductions and inferences based on an obsolete and unscientific body of thought; indeed he is suspicious of deductions of any sort that are not grounded in reliable observations.

An interesting contrast to the headman is his opponent, Simbwindimbwi, the traditional doctor, or witch doctor. Simbwindimbwi is much more impulsive than the headman, quicker to feel the "sudden noose of anger coiling inside him," as he does early in his first interview with the headman on Matenda's case. Given to an exaggerated sense of his own importance, he quickly (and wrongly) assumes that the headman has put up Musyani to complaining to the Boma that he has been slandered. He is not particularly perceptive. The headman's mood "almost verging on resignation" merely seems peculiar to him; he does not realize that the headman, far from being jealous of his importance and disliking him, really likes him, although he thinks him rather queer; and he simply refuses to accept all Simbwindimbwi's professional pronouncements, partly because of a skepticism "about almost everything." Simbwindimbwi is unable to understand why the headman will not accept his diagnosis by "deduction" of Matenda's illness or the use of his secret medicines. Of course he never understands the headman's insistence on having real, western-style, evidence. After he loses out in the modified poison ordeal, Simbwindimbwi abruptly throws all his esoteric ingredients into his cloth bag, along with his shirts. He prepares to leave the village in a huff, but before he goes he delivers a diatribe against the headman and dances a kind of choreographic denunciation, his cowbells softly jingling at his ankles. In a shouting match with the headman in front of the dying Matenda's house, he is quite out of control, while the headman is very much in command of the situation.

Mwenimuzi and Simbwindimbwi are in agreement on two points: the rudeness of modern children and the need to respect the ancient traditions of the tribe. The doctor is upset by the impoliteness of the young daughter of the Mwenimuzi's messenger as she pertly asks where the headman is, and the headman is annoyed by the schoolboy who rudely contradicts him when he maintains that the morning star and the evening star are different stars. After his first interview with the headman Simbwindimbwi stomps off outraged, accusing the headman of "parting ways with tradition." And in a way he is right, for the headman has insisted on western-style evidence and will not be satisfied with Simbwindimbwi's traditional dicta. However, Mwenimuzi does truly respect tradition. At the poison ordeal he calls upon the ancestors to help him and his people; he approves, or pretends to approve, of treating witches in accordance with "ancient custom," of "abid[ing] by the many examples left to us by antiquity." He is willing to violate the white government's prohibition against mwavi when the "security and happiness" of his people are at stake. It is true that the headman's poison ordeal is a very much modified version of the traditional rite, with modifications going far beyond the violation of protocol protested by Simbwindimbwi, and that the accuser's case is tested first. This is the difference between the two African leaders' attitudes toward tradition: Simbwindimbwi wants traditional observances to be kept totally unchanged; Mwenimuzi respects the traditional observances but wants them modified to fit modern conditions.

The principal dramatic interest concerns the hostile relations between Musyani and Matenda, his family and his doctor; and the charge of witchcraft brought against Musyani; this is the hostility with which the headman must cope. The quarrel is nicely managed by Kayira, accelerating from the original competition over a woman through the brawl at the communal beer party, Musyani's visiting the dying Matenda and his hostile family, the headman's tense interview with the doctor and the dying man's brother and son (as Musyani eavesdrops), the public meeting and symbolic poison ordeal, the angry confrontation between the headman and the doctor outside Matenda's house, Matenda's funeral and the arson committed by Sinka, Matenda's son, and Tepa, his brother. This sequence of episodes of constantly increasing hostility moves toward a climax, and each step in the steady progression of hostility is interesting in itself. The climactic development is followed by a tragicomic anticlimax, the incidents of the white men's justice: the unsuccessful comic-opera pursuit of Simbwindimbwi and the punishment of the arsonists and the headman. The reader's expectations in cause and effect are never disappointed: all the episodes are entirely plausible, although we may wonder why Matenda did not at once make clear his intentions of marrying both the orphan sisters (elder sisters must marry first?), or why the villagers and the doctor do not question the headman's substituting pigeons for the principals in the poison ordeal.

The reader may wonder about the function in the novel of Simeon the Watchtower evangelist, the homeless man with a catlike face who wears a red-buttoned yellow shirt and white trousers, and who continually harangues the villagers about hellfire and damnation and distributes pamphlets in various languages that the villagers use for cigarette paper. Since the Watchtower movement is a western phenomenon, one of the multitude of variants of Christianity, perhaps Simeon and his peculiar evangelism, like the silly military posturing of the headman's messenger, suggest the craziness and total irrelevance of many cultural imports as they appear in Africa. The other western man of God in the novel, Father Puccinni, is a good man who kindly dispenses candy to the children and cigarettes to the men, consoles the widow, and lets a child stroke his golden hair. Yet somehow we get the impression that he is also "out of it," not a power in the land, not relevant, though he reminds us that not all Europeans in Africa are brutally abrupt and self-centered.

And how does the headman's tale of the British imperialists who kidnapped his father and his men to hunt the slave-dealer Mlozi fit into the scheme of the novel? Is it meant to point up the brutality and rapaciousness of the early British agents of the civilizing mission? Or is it to foreshadow Mwenimuzi's humiliation by his father's humiliation in being kidnapped with his men, struck, tied up, and deprived of his prize bull? Most importantly, perhaps, the episode represents the ineptitude of many imperialist enterprises; the whole expedition is a farce: Mlozi is not even in the forest. Besides being brutal, callous, and unfair, the Europeans are inept; Mlozi is never in any danger from the expedition. The mention of the mountain road built by mistreated prisoners, of the prisoners mowing lawns and burying the hospital dead, and of the ridiculous custom of Africans standing when a white man sits in his office all give us glimpses of the seamier side of the great civilizing mission.

The style of this novel is notably successful: not very figurative, nor very emphatic. But in spite of being simple and plain, it is rather formal. A formal style, "distancing," is well suited to the detached manner of the novel, because the formality is spiced with Kayira's cool, ironical wit and because there is enough excitement to make stylistic piquancy unnecessary.

The Looming Shadow should win a respectable reputation in this country as one of the more interesting African-English novels. If it does not convey quite such a rich matrix of traditional cultural details as the best of Chinua Achebe's Nigerian novels, *Things Fall Apart* (1958) and *Arrow of God* (1964), it does deliver some fascinating anthropological notations on this Tumbuka-speaking people of Northern Malawi: the premises and speculations of a witch doctor, the men's communal eating hall, the poison ordeal, the mortuary customs, the high regard for cattle, the spontaneous solo dancing and the ululating to express joy, and a hint of the social hierarchy and its persons "with shadows." *The Looming Shadow* has an intensity and a dramatic power missing in most of the African biographical novels emphasizing the trials of schooling, like William Conton's *The African* (Gambia, 1960), or Amu Djoleto's *The Strange Man* (Ghana, 1967), or in the "domestic affairs" novels, like Elechi Amadi's *The Concubine* (Nigeria, 1966), or John Munonye's *The Only Son* (Nigeria, 1966). Kayira's novel has a vitality rather like that of Cyprian Ekwensi's lively novels dealing with the vigor and squalor of life in Lagos or the comic novels of T. M. Aluko about Yoruba in contact with European ideas, but Kayira is usually more apt in organization and characterization than either Ekwensi or Aluko. A reader familiar with African-English novels might well be reminded of two Nigerian novels which have something like the light touch of *The Looming Shadow*: Nkem Nwankwo's *Danda* (1964) about a ne'er-do-well who fails in both the traditional and the European modes of life, and Gabriel Okara's strangely moving symbolical novel, *The Voice,* about a young man in search of integrity who is baffled in European as well as traditional circles. Like these two fine novels Kayira's *The Looming Shadow* has a distinct freshness and originality.

HAROLD R. COLLINS

THE LOOMING
SHADOW

1

Musyani sat motionless as if screwed to his stool. He shook his head in amazement and, spitting on the dusty ground, muttered in a loud voice, "Magic! Magic!"

His partner, a short man with a face that revealed an encounter with smallpox at some period in the past, also expressed his own opinion in his own manner about the strange phenomenon of the day. Pretty soon the whole village broke into a wild charivari as women came running out of their houses with naked babies held precariously and others being dragged behind, and men, those who felt unconcerned about the meaning of it all, took to dancing, performing their steps with such intricate gestures as had never before been seen. Already the sun was being given an impromptu bombardment— a deafening chorus of tom-tom drums, cowbells, anything that could be used to make noise, as each one tried to make the loudest noise in an effort to put life in the sun. But in a few moments the whole thing was over, and the ululating women and the dancing men returned to their chores.

An eclipse of the sun was always an occasion that was greeted with mixed feelings by the population of Kavukuku Village, still caught between the light of modernity, flickering as from a distant candle, and the looming shadow of darkness left from antiquity, a reminder of their past and dictator of their present. To the young ones not yet graduated from the school of the cicada and mantis, still to master the great art of predicting the coming of the rainy season by the first spawnings of mushrooms, or the return of centipedes from their hibernation, still to understand the reasons behind the surrendering of the first harvest to the cemetery of the great ancestors, the eclipse of the sun was wonderful, exciting, and nothing more. But to the old ones, tempered by tradition, weak to challenge its occasional fallacy, nothing in their universe could be dismissed with a shrug of the shoulders, for the ordered universe never told jokes, and the death of the sun could only foretell the death of their chief or someone from that rare species of men called great.

At such times the chief, considering himself the only one of his kind and therefore the only victim of the impending calamity—as though the eclipse would affect only his village—would gather together his councilors—sometimes even ordering them in the name of the divine—to pronounce within their souls and in their own manner some honest prayers, in an attempt to flatter the supernatural power into averting its decision. Those who were considered great by others would, at such times, always humble themselves by adding in their prayers that although they were great, the chief was greater still.

The whole thing had started late one afternoon when a passerby announced that a white man had pronounced with absolute finality that there would be an eclipse of the sun the following Friday morning.

"Liar!" the chief shouted at him. The man swore to God that he had heard the words with his own two ears. The chief declared that no person had ever predicted the "death of the sun" and that he was going to detain the passerby in the village until after Friday morning, that the man was going to pay for it if he was lying.

"I hate to disobey your orders, sir," the passerby said, "but I am a prince in my own area." Saying this, he picked up his luggage and started for his home.

Friday morning the people waited impatiently for the eclipse while the village headman paced the streets with his hands at his back, looking like a pious priest saying his morning prayers. Musyani and his partner were sitting on three-legged stools forging an axe, one fanning the coals with bellows made of goat's skin and the other hitting the red-hot steel on a smooth rock with a huge hammer, each hit being unfalteringly accompanied by the sound of "Huh! Huh! Huh!" issuing from his nostrils. Then he would push the steel under the coals. It was in this setting that the eclipse found Musyani, and like many others he was more amazed at the possibility of predicting it than at the meaning of its occurrence, the latter hardly concerning him as fate had destined him to be neither chief nor great.

"Times have changed," he said, raising his head with its grizzled countenance and narrowing his big round eyes, which could change from brown to red, even when he was neither angry nor disturbed. These features, plus his long black curly beard, which he cherished and seemed to have left uncut deliberately as a compromise for the total loss of his hair, gave him not only an aging look but also a peculiar resemblance to the imaginary appearance of what they called witches, the greatest allies of the devil. Whenever children met such people, they trembled like frightened dogs and hurried home to whisper in the ears of their elders about what they had seen.

"Don't ever take anything from them," their elders would whisper back.

"Times have changed," Musyani was saying. There were times which Musyani remembered only too acutely when witches were the most disliked people in the village. Whenever some person was declared to be a witch, the whole village would gather and, following the pronouncement of the chief, would combat the devil in the person of the witch by burning his house, laying waste his belongings, or, better yet, putting his dastardly acts to an end by locking him up in his burning house. Musyani could think of nothing that offered more excitement than waiting for hours to see someone's house go ablaze and the owner disappear into useless cinders. But all this had changed, even for these traditionally minded people, and witches had found refuge in the law of the land.

Times had indeed changed. The older folks went about their business, took off their hats or fezes when they met a European and said, "Yes, Bwana!" when speaking to him, or stood at attention in a military fashion as they had seen the members of the King's African Rifles do for their white-faced officers. They went to church on Sundays, sang hymns and heard sermons, came home to dispute among themselves as to the merits of closing their eyes when praying.

"So we don't see the Lord," some would shout, grinning knowledgeably. Then they would drink.

The younger folks went about in brown sandals with

high khaki stockings, which were always folded over
at the top just below the knees. They wore starched and
neatly pressed khaki shorts whose hems were turned
up, white shirts with sleeves long or else folded up,
fountain pens proudly displayed in their shirt pockets,
black bow ties below their chins. They wore neither hats
nor fezes and always parted their hair on the left. And
they were inclined to say, "Is that so!" when talking to
a European, or, with tongue in cheek, "So what! . . .
And what does that prove?" The European, if it was a
woman, would always go away complaining that the
rascals had been spoiled.

They washed their clothes on Sunday mornings when
their elders went to church, and played football in the
afternoons when their elders discussed the day's Word
of God over a pot of beer and occasionally shouted,
"Children Respect the Sabbath!" But otherwise they
paid no attention to the witches, so the unfortunate
people who were fated to wear the looks of witches
found peace at last.

Musyani and his companion were still discussing the
eclipse, while the steel that once had been part of the
springs of an automobile was under the burning coals.
Then the steel was hot again and, after pulling it out,
the two went through the whole process again. One held
the steel on the rock with the help of a handle and the
other hit it with the hammer and, little by little, forged
it into an axe.

Presently a little boy, sucking his thumb fervently and
wearing a tattered cloth that left bare his protruding
brown belly, came and sat next to Musyani. An instant
later he moved four feet away, in response to the old
man's command. "It's hot here. Go sit under that tree."

"Did someone send you here, Gitta?" Musyani inquired.

"Yes," Gitta, the little boy, said, looking down like a shy girl as he said it. He sat motionless, wearing a serious expression on his round face as though refusing to utter any further word on that subject or any other. Occasionally he raised his eyes to the two men, quivered his lips as if to say something, then looked down again, but did not say a single word, as if determined not to impart to them the message that had brought him there, not even if they were entitled to it.

Musyani knew that he would have to extract the message from the little boy, and, mustering his patience, he proceeded.

"Who sent you?"

"Who sent me?" the boy repeated, pushing his thumb deeper into his mouth.

"Yes."

"Grandma sent me."

"Which grandma?"

"Grandma Nachele," the little boy said.

Of course Nachele was not his grandmother, but the little boy had already mastered his rules of politeness.

"Why did she send you here?"

"Why did she send me here?" the little boy repeated.

"Yes," Musyani said, but without waiting for the answer he resumed his hitting. "Huh! Huh! Huh! . . ."

"There is a man at the house," the little boy said.

Musyani pushed the steel under the coals, and his companion was at his bellows again. Now he stood the skin bag with its top open, now he pushed it down with its top shut, and the air rushed through the clay pipe into the coals, sending the smaller ones flying in all directions. The flames leaped madly as the air hit the coals, then died down, and then leaped again.

Musyani stood up and, wiping away the dark ashes from the front of his multiholed satin shorts with his

open palm, walked to the boy under the tree in a stooping gesture as though he were about to walk on all
fours.

"H'm," he sighed as he sat beside the little one. "A
man is at the house, eh! Do you know him?"

The boy shrugged his shoulders and scratched the
ground with a piece of wood.

"Grandma said you should come."

"All right," he said. "Go tell her I'm coming. We are
taking a break shortly." The little boy vanished.

Half an hour later the two men took a break. Actually it was not a break at all, as they did not intend
to resume their work until the following day. Leaving
their implements, they walked to the village, Musyani
hiding his shiny-pated head under a black fez, which he
had bargained for with an Indian, buying it for two
shillings instead of the four the Indian demanded.

The village itself, comprised of hundreds of bungal-
lows, had been carefully planned. All these bungalows
were built in sixteen straight lines, all their doors facing
in the same direction, and all the barns were built on
one side of the village, thus leaving free the other
three sides for future houses. The streets were wide and
dusty. In the middle of the village there were several
open spaces. Children played there. Old folks held their
beer parties there. The two eating places—one for the
men and the other for the women—were also located
there. On the southern end of the village there was a
church, its outer walls whitewashed, its roof higher than
most of the houses. A few yards away from the church
there was a football field. The boys, just back from
school on leave and seemingly more concerned with
their physical fitness than the salvation of their souls,
spent their Sunday mornings and afternoons playing
football in that field. Most of these boys built their own

houses at the end of the streets while most of the girls slept either with their grandmothers or with such widows as their parents or the old men in the village approved. The village life was such that almost everyone knew his place.

The village at this hour was almost always deserted. The people were all out doing their chores, and they would not come back until the evening, when the village would return to its normal life, with the shouting of the happy children and the singing and dancing of the old folks at their regular beer parties. At this early afternoon hour all would be quiet and tranquil. Even the chickens, tired and uninterested in scratching the ground any more, would sit dreamily under the trees or on verandas. Occasionally smoke would creep out of one or the other of the hundreds of bungalows, all monotonously similar. Slowly it would rise in curls to the high blue ceiling of the sky, there to float and disappear.

However, on this particular day the village was not completely deserted. Nachele was home. At the other end of one of the streets a few people were sitting and lying lazily in the shade in front of a house, still talking about the eclipse. The white man, they were saying, had made it. How else could he have predicted it? The white men, they all agreed, had gone very deep with their magic. A few goats together with some calves were loitering about, running loose around the houses, and one goat, wearing a long beard, came running past the two men, followed by a barking dog.

Musyani recognized at once the man sitting on the veranda of his house. It was Chande from down the street, wearing his long black beard that was not unlike the goat's.

"It's a hot day," Musyani said as he squatted beside

the other man. "One would wish it would rain. Do they have any drink anywhere today?"

"Not that I know of," Chande said. "There may be some tomorrow, but I am not really sure."

The two men exchanged some words on various topics, including the inevitable eclipse, then Musyani's wife, Nachele, came out of the house carrying a broom in her hand.

"I am not going to detain you any further," Chande said, "but—"

"Not at all," Musyani quickly interrupted. "I am in no hurry. It's too hot to do anything right now. I only wish I could get something with which to wet my throat."

"Yes, indeed," Chande said softly. "You would think our women have forgotten how to brew."

"We are too busy," Nachele said in defense of her sex.

"Busy," Musyani muttered savagely. "Busy!"

There ensued a deathlike silence save for the rustle of wind and leaves in the background. The two men stole quick glances at each other as if to weigh each other, to determine what was currently running in each other's mind. Musyani thought of asking Chande what it was that had brought him there, but he decided against it as he considered it impolite to do so. "If it's important," he said to himself, "he will say it."

"Could I speak to you in private?" Chande asked softly and politely but with a cunning expression on his face that quickly evoked Musyani's suspicions.

"By all means," Musyani said. "Let us step into the house."

"The house is rather dirty," Nachele said. "I was just going to sweep it."

The two men ignored her and proceeded to enter

the house, with Musyani leading the way and Chande leaving the door behind him half-open. Nachele remained sitting outside.

The floor was dusty as the good woman had said. Chande took a quick look at the room. Along the wall opposite the door there was a row of black pots, each one with a lid on top. In one corner, a relatively dark place, a chicken sat on its eggs, occasionally issuing a snoring-like sound as if in a dream. From another room emanated a constant but faint hissing sound, as if from some distant ravaging storm. It was coming from a small pot—also with a lid—that sat on a dying fire. Nachele was baking some beans. Over the fire-place and suspended from the rafters were two ball-like things made of leaves which contained Nachele's store of canned mushrooms and vegetables. In the wet season, when there was an abundance of mushrooms and green vegetables, she would boil and dry them. Then she would wrap them in leaves and store them over the fireplace, where they would be free from moss and decay. In another corner, diagonally opposite the fire-place, a big membrane was smeared on the wall. Over it, and in several other places, cobwebs, dexterously woven and interwoven, hung like nests.

The two men sat on stools, facing each other. Chande sighed deeply, as if to say, "It's hopeless!" Musyani looked at his visitor's face. It looked ominous. Then he thought he felt a slight twitch in his own eyes. He looked down.

"Matenda is quite ill," Chande said.

"Yes," Musyani said. "Nachele told me last night, and I have been meaning to go and see him this afternoon."

"His brother, Tepa, and his son, Sinka, are both there at his house."

"Oh, yes, I thought I saw both of them this afternoon," Musyani said. He said a few more words, then stopped, realizing that what he was saying was not exactly true, that really he had not seen either Tepa or Sinka that afternoon.

"They have sent me to you," Chande said.

"H'm! In connection with Matenda, I suppose."

"Yes. You see, Musyani," he said, then hesitated. He was not sure how to say it. He cleared his throat and proceeded. "You see, they consulted three doctors, including Simbwindimbwi the great, these past two days, and all the doctors have singled you out as the one who has bewitched Matenda, and—"

Musyani had pricked up his ears. "Me!" he screamed, with such a frown on his face that one would have thought that it was he who had been bewitched. Had they deceived him, by any chance? His right forefinger was firmly planted on his chest, his mouth was half-open, and his eyes hung in his face unwinkingly. He remained in this posture for a whole minute. His heart thumped, throbbed, knocked, and quickened its pace. "Me!" he muttered. "How so . . . How can they . . ."

Chande sighed. It was not so difficult after all.

"I can't answer any questions," he said. "I am only a messenger and I can only tell you what they sent me to tell you."

"How can they say such a ridiculous thing?" Musyani was saying, now furious.

"I don't know, but apparently the doctors, all three of them, say you are the man."

"I am not," Musyani protested. "How can I be? I am not."

"As I said," Chande continued, "I don't know anything about these matters, and I am sorry that I don't have any details. I am only a messenger, you see. But they say, specifically Sinka, that you must cure him, that if he dies, they are going to fight back and they seem to be sure that you and your family will follow him to the grave in no time at all," he said, making a quick motion with his hand as he repeated, "in no time at all."

"But how can I cure him if I did not bewitch him?" Musyani asked, his clenched first tapping on the floor with each syllable of "I did not bewitch him."

"This is all they asked me to tell you. I have nothing more."

"They can't say that," he was now saying at the top of his voice. "No one in my family—my father, my grandfather—no one was ever accused of being a witch. Ours has been a very honorable and respectable family, and how dare they say that I bewitched Matenda? Me! Huh!"

"Oh, yes," Chande said, "there is one thing more. They say that this is between you and them. Nobody else besides you three, the doctors and myself, knows anything about this yet. If you decide to cure him of his illness, do so without making a fuss about it, and the sooner the better. If any word leaks out, people are likely to misinterpret it, you know. But if, on the other hand, you don't want to cure him, they will make a public matter of it. They are going to let the whole world know that you are a witch, and you know what that means."

"I see that you too don't believe me, but I swear upon my father's grave that I did not bewitch him, and how then can I cure him? Believe me, I am neither a witch nor a doctor."

"I don't know." Chande shrugged his shoulders. "How do people become witches?" Chande asked savagely. "I don't think they are born witches." He clapped his hands lightly and politely, signaling to the other that he was about to take leave of him. "Stay well," he said and marched out.

In the meantime Musyani was agitated, excited, and furious. He started pacing the floor from one corner to another in rapid darts, muttering between his teeth, "Ridiculous, outrageous . . . I am going to punish them for this . . ." He headed for the other corner and with one kick sent the chicken cackling out in terror.

"Stop that," Nachele said. "See, you have broken the eggs."

"Shut up . . . I am going to punish them, the doctors and all," he said, banging the wall with his bare fist.

"Watch where you step," she said.

He picked up some old newspapers, which he used for rolling his own cigarettes, and wiped the egg-things off his foot.

"Where is Nanyambo?" he wanted to know.

"How should I know?" Nachele answered. "She mentioned going to the well to see Matenda."

"Tell her not to," he commanded. "You are not to see Matenda, you hear? I am going to punish them first."

Without saying a word Nachele began sweeping the house. Musyani reached behind one of the pots and pulled out a malimba. Then he moved his stool against the wall and sat on it, leaned back and played the malimba.

A witch! That's an insult, a grave insult!

For a long time that night he lay on his mat without sleeping. He thought of many things, about what he was going to do or what was going to be done to him. He had always wondered what witches were really like. Now he was one, or at any rate they said he was one. When he was a child, his elders had told him that witches turned into owls at nights and flew anywhere they wanted. He looked around his shoulders that night to see if he was growing any wings. None. He sighed repeatedly, even began to sweat profusely. He wished he had been dreaming, but the whole thing was real, clear as day, yes indeed, clear as the little fire still flickering in the corner of the dark room, a halo in its own right, a true *lux in tenebris.*

It was no secret that Musyani Mtambo and Matenda Nyondo had not, for a number of years, been on what one would call good terms. Indeed, far from it, for they had made it a habit to fight each other publicly at every conceivable opportunity, and they always denounced each other in private, saying, "I will kill him!"

Their dispute was nothing new, since it was not entirely peculiar to the two men. In short, it was a common one, having its roots in women—two sisters to be specific. There was an eighteen-year girl called Nasama, and her sister, Nachele, who was two years younger. The two sisters had suddenly found themselves orphaned, their father having died of a snake bite one afternoon and their mother having died only a few days later of the same cause. The two incidents, although removed from each other in time, still remained so similar as to perpetuate the growing myth that the family had been bewitched. Why, for instance, would the reptile attack a man now and his wife a few days later?

The orphaned sisters lived in what had been their

parents' house, a bungalow like the other houses in the village. Surmising that he would not have to pay much dowry since the girls' parents were dead, Matenda vowed to himself that he was going to marry both and immediately took a pretended fancy for the older one.

One dark, cold, and windy night in July, Matenda found himself standing at the door of Nasama's house, shivering and waiting. Earlier that day they had agreed to meet there at that outrageous hour of the night. Slowly the door opened and an indistinct figure appeared, seemed to hesitate until Matenda was able to whisper, "I am here." He eloped with Nasama and fled the village with the speed of an eagle, leaving the sleeping sister behind. Nachele, unable to comprehend the situation when her sister failed to show up all day the following day, started crying and the old men of the village, who knew the facts, took time to assure her that her sister would return. Indeed, one morning a week later Nasama and Matenda appeared in the village and declared themselves married. Then they left, along with Nachele, for Matenda's home. Matenda lived in the Chipakama Village, situated a score of miles away in a little valley, flanked on the west and the east by a range of mountains.

Matenda built Nachele a one-room bungalow next to his own house, which was also a bungalow but much bigger. Nachele had never been the sole owner of a house before, and although this was smaller than the one she and her sister had occupied before Nasama married Matenda, she never was as proud of that one as she was now. She kept it neat and clean. She swept it every morning. Once a week she smeared the entire floor with a solution of some special dirt and as soon as it was dry she polished it by gently rubbing the surface with a smooth stone which she kept for that purpose. She would not stop until the floor looked as if it were cemented and waxed, and then she trod on it with her little feet, gently and carefully like a cat. She white-washed the upper portion of the wall on the outside of the house and painted the bottom in black. The inside walls were all in white, except that part directly over the fireplace which she never washed, so that it remained brown. On several parts of the wall she had drawn pictures of a man, a dog, some pots in red paint, and a snake which had stripes of red, white, and black, re-sembling a puff adder. The man in the picture was raising a stick, but he was on the wall opposite the snake so that it could not be supposed that he was intending to beat it.

Along one of the walls, there was a wooden bed which Nachele had Matenda make for her. (He never made any for himself, and he and Nasama slept on a mat of reeds spread on the floor.) Along another wall, there was a row of pots, something that was never missing in any house that had a woman. Over the bed she had planted a nail in the wall and from it hung strings of colorful beads which Matenda had also bought for her.

As time passed, Matenda, himself haggard and in-clined to drink, became more and more attracted to Nachele, first because of her order, and then because of herself.

One afternoon his wife asked him, insinuatingly, if he knew where Nachele was at that particular moment, and he retorted, "Am I her keeper?" He was making a hoe handle at the time and continued doing so as he said this. Nasama said she did not think so, but then she went on to say that she was rather concerned that Nachele was receiving undue attention from "someone," to which he replied, "You are imagining things," and dismissed the matter.

But deep in his soul he knew that she was not just imagining things, that he coveted Nachele, coveted the thought of owning her, of calling her his wife. He longed for her always. She was young. Her kinky hair was tidy. He longed for her even white teeth behind the thick lips, her innocent brown eyes whose sparkle was life itself, the very embodiment of beauty. He wished to touch her delicate dark hands, placed at her hips as she stood to admire the white and black wall of her house. He would imagine himself running his fingers through the colorful strings of beads around her neck. She was his, she was his responsibility, and who would have the nerve to take her away from him? It was he or no one, he would say to himself and often he would confirm his decision by shaking his fist savagely at the empty space before him.

One evening he sat in Nachele's house. He just sat there, all alone, as Nachele was with Nasama. There was a fire glowing next to the wall, and he sat on a stool in front of it. The door was closed. From time to time he stretched his legs while still seated. Once in a while he reached into the pocket on his shirt and pulled out a tiny little bottle in which he stored his powdered tobacco. He opened it slowly and poured the brown stuff on his left palm and sniffed it. He groaned for a moment, feeling an immense pleasure in groaning. Tears glittered on his cheeks. His mouth half-opened automatically. An itching sensation rushed through the inside of his nose and he nearly sneezed, but the tingling sensation that had worked its way almost up to a climax died away, quietly, slowly, receding into the back of his head and out, out through the wall, or the roof maybe. He sighed with more fury than relief, spitting on the fire. He then closed his bottle and put it back into the pocket.

It was about ten o'clock when Nachele returned. He could hear her as she came running, but he did not move an inch. He just sat there. She pushed the door open and entered hastily, only to stop abruptly with a shout of "Oh!"

"Why, did I frighten you?" he said as calmly as he could.

"No," she said, "not really, but what are you doing here?"

She left the door open and went and sat at the foot of the bed, which, by reason of the size of the room, was not many feet away from the fireplace where Matenda was sitting with all the airs of self-confidence. There was silence for a few moments, and the embarrassed young woman was already thinking of returning to her sister's house and waiting there until he decided to leave on his own accord. But he went out, only to return a few moments later, closing the door behind him.

"No, I like it better this way," he said in response to her plea of, "Please leave the door open." They almost bumped into each other as the girl ran to the door and he to the foot of the bed. He had her arm in his grip before she got to the door, tried to assure her in a whisper that he did not intend to hurt her, but she turned around and bit him hard and frantically.

"What do you want here? I'll scream. I'll yell. Help! Help!"

He opened the door and flew out.

"What do you thing you are doing here?" his wife, who had already reached her sister's door, demanded.

He did not answer but walked straight to his house.

Another man came running, his blanket carelessly thrown over his shoulder, a spear in hand.

"Well!" he gasped. "I thought I heard someone cry for help. H'm. Strange . . ." he mumbled to himself as he retraced his steps and went back to his own house.

"Nothing," Matenda replied to Nasama's proddings. "What do you think I was doing there?"

They quarreled until he shouted at the top of his voice, "Shut up!"

The next day and for a whole week thereafter, Matenda was the talk of the village. Even little children repeated that he was a dirty man who broke into his sister-in-law's house. Matenda, thoroughly ashamed, became very polite in his discourses with others, something he was not accustomed to do. When he returned to his house he and Nasama only frowned at each other. He saw Nachele at close range only once or twice a day, when she brought water to his wife, who was now expecting a baby.

At the suggestion of Nachele, a group of leading men in the village conferred privately with Matenda and told him quite frankly that the young woman wished him to put an end to his clandestine behavior, that he should not take advantage of the fact that she was living under his care, and that although she loved him as a brother-in-law she had no intention whatsoever of calling him husband. She would, they told him, take him before the tribunal if he did not change his behavior. The visitors, most of whom were also members of the tribunal, said that in their opinion he must realize now once and for all that she was free to choose her own man, and that if she did not choose him, as she had already implied, he might as well forget her. However, they went on to say, he must continue to look after her until such time as she got married. Matenda promised he would do as advised.

But no sooner had his wife borne him their first child, a boy named Sinka, than he resumed his maneuvering, although this time secretly and restricted to a stare or a glance which more often than not was reciprocated by a rude sneer from the young woman. He saw her more often now since his wife, being unclean by reason of her having given birth so recently, could not cook. Moreover, custom absolutely forbade Nasama from getting out of the house with her baby in its first week. Nachele had to cook for the family, sweep her sister's house, draw water and fetch wood for her.

Matenda's objective now was not to approach Nachele as he had before. This he realized was out of the question. He was more interested in preventing any other man from seeing her so that in the long run she would bow before him and announce candidly that marrying him was preferable to remaining a spinster, an old maid. He could not, of course, build a fortification around her which would prevent men from ever coming to see her, but he could keep an eye on her himself. He could follow her to the forest when she went to fetch wood. He could follow her to the well when she went to draw water. Sometimes he would wake at odd hours of the night and walk around her house, stopping at the door to listen if she was awake. At such times he would hold his head close to the door, and with his ears pricked up, his breath held back, he would listen. Is she, by any chance, awake? Is there a man with her? He would stand there for a considerable length of time and when satisfied that she was not awake, that she did not have a man there with her, he would tiptoe back to his house.

But the young woman had her own plans. When Matenda was out one week on some errand, Musyani, a young man living with his uncle in the same village, took advantage of the other's absence and in a way not entirely original with him came in the darkness of the night, again in July, and eloped with Nachele, returning

to the village a week later. The village headman, afraid
that the two men might fight and maybe even kill each
other, took the trouble to wag his finger at Matenda,
after the latter had returned from his errand, and warn
him of the consequences if he tried to interfere with
the young couple.

But the seed of animosity, and hatred, between the
two men had been sown. They frowned at each other
like dogs. They never went into each other's house.
When they met on the street, one turned this way and
the other that way with sneers of contempt on their
faces.

They ate together, however, since men ate their meals
in common—and women too, though in a separate place
—near the headman's house. The women prepared the
food in their respective houses and the little boys carried
it to the place where the men would congregate at meal-
time. With respect to beer, men and women drank
together. But even at mealtimes, the two men would
sneer at each other, holding their food as if intending
to throw it at the other. In point of fact, Matenda
once threw his leavings. It was not determined whether
he deliberately aimed at Musyani. He himself swore that
he mean to throw the food to a dog that was squatting
behind Musyani. He even said, "I beg your pardon!"
When the breadlike lump splashed just above the
other's eye. Although Musyani publicly dismissed this
action by accepting the other's explanation that it was
an accident, he kept wondering why, if Matenda
meant to throw food at the dog, he had hit him in the
face.

3

Three years passed and the two men did not make peace. Each denounced the other in the other's absence. In the meantime, something happened which, although it did not have any direct effect upon their relations, turned out in the end to be the fuse that was to dynamite their hatred for each other.

Matenda had another child, a boy who lived for only a year, and it was whispered that Musyani had bewitched the little thing, but nothing came of it. Musyani himself, however, still did not have any children. For a long time he wondered and speculated. Finally, driven by his morbid superstition, he concluded that it was Matenda's fault that his wife did not bear and proceeded to consult several doctors, laying before each one of them what he called facts and asking each one to verify them. Each of the doctors refused to have words put in his mouth and—as if they had conferred with one another—declared that the fault lay with Musyani's dead father, who, so they said, was angry because Musyani neglected to give him beer.

For a whole month thereafter, with a calabash of beer in one hand, Musyani would grope his way to the graveyard every night, observing all sorts of strange rituals on the way such as walking backward and forward every seven steps. Once in the graveyard, he would sit down to entertain his deceased father with a beer party, pouring a portion of it on the grave and leaving the rest in the calabash there on the grave.

A year passed and nothing happened. Musyani consulted only one doctor this time and when this one told him the same thing, he sprang to his feet and declared ferociously, "I suppose they don't make any beer up there in heaven. Beer, every day beer. That swine! He must learn how to brew his own . . ."

"Don't speak like that," the alarmed doctor was begging. "You only make him more angry that way."

"Let him be," Musyani said. "I will not give him another drop."

Deciding, as most men are likely to do in similar circumstances, that his wife's sterility—he now regarded her as sterile—was either her fault or Matenda's and certainly not his, and wishing to prove to all that this was so, he married another woman, Nanyambo, a widow with a child. He knew all too well that it was a great gamble on his part to marry a woman who had tangible proof that she could bear, for if she failed to have a child by him, everyone would surely know that it was he who was barren. A year passed, then another, but no issue. He began consulting doctors again. He drank all sorts of medicines, bathed in medicinal waters, wore small roots around his neck, buried herbs under his bed at the doctor's recommendations, placed a calabash of beer at his father's grave every single night. Neither Nachele nor Nanyambo had a child.

Then one late afternoon some two hundred men and

women, comprising about half the population of the village, gathered for a beer feast to end officially a mourning period, there having been a funeral two weeks earlier. Among those attending, besides men like Musyani and Matenda, were such notables as the village headman in his full regalia, a multicolored robe, and Simbwindimbwi himself, the greatest of the tribal doctors.

There had been some showers earlier in the day, accompanied by a rather fierce thunderstorm, and the ground was still damp and smelling of rain. Now the sky was clear and the day quiet.

There were five great pots of beer and five mammoth fires burning in five different places out in the compound, and the people divided themselves into five groups, each group having a pot and a fire to itself. The compound in question was a square, reserved entirely for the purposes of beer feasts. The people sat there, their pots in front of them, each group drinking from a common pot with individual straws. They sat with their legs tucked in, some speaking and waving their straws to emphasize their points, some dancing and others clapping their hands while the women ululated. It was all happiness and joy despite the fact that they were celebrating the end of a funeral or mourning period.

Suddenly Simbwindimbwi, who had been quiet all the time, and apparently in poor spirits, began to shake his head, at first only slightly, then more and more violently, his mouth foaming, his legs trembling, then his body and his hands. He was sighing, smiling like a child. His teeth began to chatter as from cold. Then he was beating his chest and burping, tears glittering on his cheeks, then sobbing helplessly. Startled, the entire assemblage stared at him with faces that bore ex-

pressions of revulsion. Each person started searching
his own soul feverishly, wondering if the doctor, the all-
knowing Simbwindimbwi, would call upon him and
publicly reveal his secret deeds. Mwenimuzi, the village
headman, stood up to say something and the serious
expression on his face suggested that he was about to
say something of the utmost importance. But he was
interrupted by Simbwindimbwi, who was now hopping
around the fire on one leg, still sighing deeply and burping now and then, beating his chest with his hands, with
tears running down his cheeks. He stopped just a few
feet away from Musyani. Raising his big hands in the
air, his morose eyes fixed on the ground—with the
crowd absolutely quiet and motionless as if striken—
he began singing the alma mater of his profession:

Zilimumo mwe, sengo he,
Zilimumo mwe, sengo he,
Zilimumo mwe, zilimumo mwe, sengo mwe.
(The witches' horns are just around the corner.)

Then he burped some more and fell to the wet
ground, where he began rolling his body. Matenda
sprang to his feet and, pointing his finger accusingly at
Musyani, shouted, "You are a witch! Yes, you are, or
why would he have stopped near you?"

The crowd stirred and presently went into a guffaw,
roared with such a frenzy of laughter that the headman's words of reprimand were completely swallowed
up. But Matenda in an absolute stupor, his tongue sticking out of his mouth, bent forward and wagging his
finger, and a pale smile on his drink-ravaged face, was
slowly advancing toward the other man. "Ah! You are a
witch."

Meanwhile Simbwindimbwi, still burping and heaving great sighs, jumped to his feet and fled to the forest, where he disappeared behind the trees with their new green leaves, and only the tinkling of the cowbells about his ankles could be heard as he ran. A few minutes later he reappeared, his eyes now doubly dilated, bunches of leaves in both hands while he chewed on others.

Perhaps, in order to convey the impression that he did not attach any importance to Matenda's rancorous words, Musyani was laughing with the crowd at the drunkard.

"Ah! You are a witch," Matenda was repeating, slowly advancing.

Simbwindimbwi was running around the fires again, spitting out the leaves and throwing the others onto the fire.

"You are a witch, not a man. That's why you don't bear children . . ."

Musyani, beginning to feel insulted and appalled at the other's behavior, wrung his fists in profound exasperation. He sprang to his feet and picked up a calabash containing hot water.

"Come on," he said. "Make one more move forward and I swear I will break this on your head."

"Put it down at once!" Mwenimuzi, the headman, was finally heard. He swung his right hand encircled with its big white bracelet made from an elephant's tusk. "Put down the calabash, at once!"

Musyani put it down as commanded.

"And you! Go sit down or I will fine you fifteen shillings for that."

"You are a witch! A witch!" Matenda insisted, slowly advancing on Musyani.

Musyani picked up the calabash again and, without announcing his intentions, threw it at his tormentor. It landed on Matenda's feet and splashed them with hot water. "I will kill you one of these days," Musyani said.

Matenda turned pale and, as if collapsing, fell on the ground.

"Did you hear him?" he cried. "Did you hear him? He says he's going to kill me . . . He's going to kill me . . ."

"For that, Musyani," the headman shouted, "I am fining you one pound. And as for you, Matenda—" The poor man had fainted. "Get going, all of you. Back to your houses. No more drinking!"

Two men carried Matenda into his house. The others reluctantly dispersed, complaining that it was without logic that they should be stopped from drinking their beer because of those two rascals.

Musyani walked to his house, still wringing his hands, his mouth compressed.

4

Usually Musyani got up before sunrise, and long before his wives did. Often, after getting dressed, he would open the door and let his chickens out of the house into the vast empty pasture land, where they could resume their scratching.

But that morning, sunrise found him asleep in bed. His assistant at the bellows had knocked at the door, and upon Nachele's assurance that the blacksmith was not in any mood to work that day, he had walked back to his house to devise other plans. It was not until eight o'clock that Musyani rose, and even then it was only because Nachele woke him. She had to sweep the house before the headman's sanitary men arrived for their regular rounds of inspection. Musyani got up, wryly puckered his big eyes. His enormous hands stretched out to the accompaniment of a deep yawn, which brought tears to his eyes. He put on the khaki shorts and shirt that he always wore—sometimes for a stretch of several months.

He felt an acute pain in his head and, realizing that

he had missed his supper the previous evening, asked his wife if there was anything left for him to eat. There was nothing, she said, but she would prepare something.

"It's all right," he said and resigned himself to grinding his teeth in silent anger.

He went out to the bathhouse, a small screen behind the house, where Nachele always put for him a basin of hot water, which she heated on an open fire each morning that he slept in her house. He only rinsed his mouth. This done, he went into Nanyambo's house to say good-day to his second wife and to give her orders. He came back to Nachele's house and told her what he had just told the other woman, which, in short, was that he, Musyani, was going to see Matenda and that, until further notice, the two women were not to go and see the ailing man.

This was in June, three months after Matenda's dramatic hysterics at the beer feast. Since then his health had been steadily declining. A week previously he had begun to hallucinate, moan and groan miserably, and had frantic convulsions day in and day out. While in these fits he screamed and cried and mentioned all kinds of names, some unheard of before, saying that these people were constantly tormenting him.

"Take them away! Take them away!" he would cry and at such times his attendants would hold him down on his mat for fear that he might hurt himself.

Musyani walked down the street on his way to Matenda's. From the dry looks of the ground, the absence of clouds in the sky, and the soft breeze coming down from the mountains, he knew that the dry season was only around the corner. For another four or five months there would be neither hoeing nor planting but only dancing and drinking. He passed one house, then another, and at the third he overheard a woman giving advice to her children.

"I want you, children, to listen very carefully," the woman was saying. "Don't accept any food from Nachele or Nanyambo."

"Liar!" he said with vexation. As he approached another house he saw Gitta, the little boy, jumping up and down. Gitta dashed into the house before Musyani got there, and Musyani was convinced that the boy had done so after seeing him. "Absolutely!" he muttered. A few more children were playing in the yard, drawing animals and the like on the ground. They only smiled instead of saying their usual "Good-day, Grandpa." He concluded that Chande must have been lying, that the whole village had already judged him a witch.

In front of Matenda's house, Nasama and four men, some relations of the ailing man, were basking in the morning sun. They were sitting in single file with their backs turned against the sun, the men with their legs tucked under in a way reminiscent of the Turks. With their chins high and their hands folded and resting in their laps, they looked like four Buddhas facing west. They were engaged in a discussion which they stopped when they saw Musyani approaching. They remained silent as he came up to them, then one of the men bellowed out with a strange politeness, delivered in a harsh voice, "Welcome, Musyani!"

"Eh! eh!" responded Musyani, who was now bent in an extended bow, Japanese style, his fez pressed under his arm and clapping his hands. "Eh, my lords!"

As if he were a plane preparing to land, he slowed down and quickly surveyed the area, then sat down directly in front of them, tucked in his feet in the usual manner, and, offering another deep bow, as if paying homage to the four Buddhas and their female companion, inquired, "And how did we sleep last night?"

Nasama, who was regarding the newcomer, issued a
sonorous "H'm!" and then remained silent for a few
moments, her pale eyes narrowed and concentrating on
a lone ant that was foraging about.

"Sleep?" she said. "H'm! Can we sleep? Shall the day
come when we shall also toss ourselves on the mat,
sigh with relief, and sleep?" She spoke softly but as one
who is about to explode into tears. Musyani, in the
meantime, assumed an expression of total gloom.

"No," she continued, shaking her little head as she
said it. "No, we shall never sleep. Others may, but
not us. You see, there has been no change in his condition, and last night, like the one before, he moaned
and groaned and foamed incessantly. Thanks to your
prayers we went through one more night! Eh . . ."

"Tut! Tut! Tut!" Musyani was also shaking his
head. "You don't say! How terrible! We must keep on
praying. May God bless His innocent and weak creatures!"

The four Buddhas braced themselves and their
mouths twitched at the corners. They looked at Musyani with pellucid eyes, wearing an expression of
amazement, as though they did not believe him. Musyani was now posing as the fifth Buddha, right in
front of them.

Nasama, who all this time had been sitting with her
legs stretched out and pressed against each other,
raised one gently and carefully like a lady enamored
with decency and placed it over the other, resting her
hands with interlocked fingers limpidly in her lap. For
a moment their mutual attention was centered on a hen
that was being pursued by a big black cock. Because of
its big red combs and white sickle feathers, the cock
was of the species generally called European. Thus it

was always associated with the white man. The implication was that if a white man were a cock, he would do exactly the same thing. As if imploring the deities to come to her defense, the hen stopped right between Musyani and the others. But Musyani dismissed the hen with a swing of his hand and shouted, "Away!"

"May the Lord curse all witches," Musyani resumed the conversation. "We are poor honest people. We don't steal anybody's things. We don't curse any person. We help the poor. What is it that we don't do right?" He was now waving his hands gently and politely to emphasize his words, and he continued to moralize. "What I don't understand is why the witches pick on us, leaving free the thugs, the dishonest, the immoral. H'm. Why?" He stopped, flushing, and scrutinized the others with curiosity. "Exactly," he began again. "Exactly, what are the witches after? In particular, why us?"

"Is he preaching?" One man whispered in the ear of the man on his right.

"Ach, for all I know!" the other whispered back with a shrug of the shoulders.

"Could *we* smoke with you?" the first whisperer asked with a faint smile, revealing for a moment that one of his front upper teeth was missing.

"Oh, sure," Musyani said. "I don't have a paper, though." He pulled out his tobacco bag made of cloth and passed it to the fellow, who, after taking his fill, returned the bag to the owner and set about rolling his cigarette with a dry maize-leaf for want of a paper.

"It's in our blood," Nasama said. "It's in our blood to be hated, to be picked on by the witches, and no matter how much good we may do to others, we shall still be hated. The witches, they suck your blood and when your blood is sweet, how can they spare you? You may say to them, 'But I am a good person!' and they will say, 'Oh yes, you are a good person, better even than so-and-so, but your blood is also sweeter!' So they bewitch you, they suck your blood and finally, after tormenting and agonizing you, they kill you. God? Wouldn't He have put a stop to it long ago if He disapproved of it?"

"That's very true," Musyani said. A fly buzzed over and settled on his head. He whisked it off with his open palm, then unconsciously his hand touched his fez, which was lying on the ground beside him. He withdrew the hand.

"There's a rumor going around now," he said. "Such a rumor is hazardous and can only benefit those who want to injure our ailing friend. You see, my good sister," he continued, ruling out the in-law bit, "they will take advantage of it. They will continue their evil works, hiding behind the innocent person whom they persuade the people to condemn as a witch. That's how cunning they are. All they need is a scapegoat, and once this is furnished, they will merely sit down and plan on their next victim just as vultures dream of a dead corpse, though it is miles away."

The man with the missing tooth was now smoking his cigarlike cigarette, which smelled more like dead pine needles than tobacco. He had not been very sure of Musyani's use of the word "us." He wanted to ask him what he meant, but he thought the others would think he was only trying to be profound. Instead he said, "You ask, 'Why us?' I will say this. First of all, you have to acknowledge the fact that they, the witches, are themselves wicked, infidels if you like, and as such you wouldn't expect them to spare the good and strike the wicked, would you?"

He took another puff of his cigarette and breathed out the stench with the air of a man proud of the smooth flow of his logic. "Have you ever seen black magic, Musyani?" he asked poignantly.

"Where would I?" Musyani answered brusquely, with an expression of grave annoyance on his face. "Like the rest of us here, I only hear about it."

The man with the missing tooth winked at the man on his right as to say, "He's lying!"

"I suppose," Musyani said, "I can go in and see Matenda."

"Yes," Nasama said. "The doctor and the others are in there now."

So the doctor had been summoned to see the patient, Musyani thought. From the title "doctor" he knew at once that it was Simbwindimbwi, otherwise Nasama would have referred to him by his full name. It must be difficult to be a doctor, traveling miles and miles to visit patients.

"I shall be going in shortly," Nasama said. "If you want, you can wait until then." Musyani said he would wait.

Then he began wondering why it was that there were no doctors living in this village, why all the neighboring villages had doctors but not this one. Precisely at that moment, as if his ears had suddenly opened, corrected after a long period of deafness, he heard the following conversation coming from inside the house:

"This is a very unusual case," Simbwindimbwi, the doctor, was saying. "I have traveled far and wide and God knows how many patients I have seen but, to be frank with you, my good fellows, this is the most unique, most unusual case that I have ever come across."

"Would you say there is any possibility of having him unwitched?" someone asked in a dead tone.

"I don't know," the doctor said. "I can say this,

though, that the poison"——he preferred to call it poison
—"which he has used in bewitching our friend here
is entirely strange to me. Although I cannot speak for
them, I am sure my colleagues would agree with me in
this. The trouble is that this poison does not act according to any laws and disobeys all the laws we know.
When I came into the house earlier this morning, I asked
him which part of his body was in pain, and you all
heard what he said. He said that at that particular
moment it was his armpits but that it changed from time
to time. The pain would be in his head, then it would
go to his heart, which would knock and knock. It
would go down to the toes or to the fingers or up into
his mouth or the neck and his arms would become
numb. Now, what kind of disease is that? The very fact
that it constantly changes positions makes it doubly
difficult to combat. And as you know, it doesn't follow
any pattern at all in its change.

"I could, for example, give him medicine for his
headache, but no sooner would I do it than the pain
would move down to, say, the heart, and by the time
I got down to the heart, it would be in his mouth or
some other place and this would go on endlessly. Of
course, and I don't need to remind you of this, it would
be fatal to administer all these medicines at once.

"As far as I can make anything out of this general
confusion, I think the witch has used a very novel
idea. You see, what he had done is simply that he has
put a living evil spirit in our friend's body and this
is what is making all the difference. It is not that the
poison he has used is extraordinarily powerful so that
it cannot be treated. It is because it is in the form of
a living spirit. It may or may not reason, but apparently
it thinks.

"Why do I say that? Well, it has to think to be able

to do what it is doing, and by thinking it knows. Yes, it knows that if it stayed in one place any self-respecting doctor would destroy it, or that if it changed positions according to some regular pattern, it wouldn't take long for a doctor to determine the pattern and so destroy it all the same. So it has chosen to do neither of these."

"I suppose then that only the witch himself would be able to destroy this spirit of his creation," the other person said.

"He may or he may not," the doctor said. "I said a moment ago that he has used a very novel idea and that I have never encountered this sort of disease anywhere else before. Obviously he has not used this spell on any other person before. Most likely he has used it in this particular case as an experiment and the very fact that it is an experiment should indicate to you or anybody else here that he, too, is not exactly sure whether or not he can destroy it."

"Since this is an experiment," another person said, "we can expect him to try to stop it, destroy it, that is, just for the sake of assuring himself that he has control over his creation."

"No," the doctor said. "You are mishandling the mind of a witch. You must realize that his foremost objective is, if not to torment his victim to the last degree, to kill him and he would be satisfied with his experiment if his objective was achieved."

"There's no hope, then," the same person said.

"We won't know for some time," the doctor said. "You see, I have planted these two little horns on his arms, one on each. It's a little experiment which I am trying. You saw me make a couple of cuts on his arms and then, after sticking these little empty horns over the wounds, I began sucking and then closed the open ends of the horns with this beeswax. What I am trying to do is simply this: since this spirit moves, as we have said, chances are that it is carried by blood or, at any rate, moves through the veins. Matenda has said that sometimes the pain is in his fingers, right? In order to get there, it must travel through the arms, and what I am hoping to accomplish by this experiment of mine is that the poison may be sucked into the horns and that will be the end of it!"

"In other words," the other person said, "in other words, the horns are still sucking the blood as they are standing there."

"That's it," the doctor said. "I closed the open ends and so set them to work on their own."

Nasama, who had been listening to the conversation, stood up and was about to go into the house. The four Buddhas excused themselves, saying they were going out into the forest to cut some trees to use for building their barns. Musyani picked up his fez and stood behind Nasama, who was to lead him into the house. The sun had grown hotter as it approached its zenith, and the four men decided that they might as well wait to cut wood until sometime in the afternoon when it would be cooler. They walked back to their houses and Nasama and Musyani went into the house.

The house, a bungalow like all the others in the village, had two rooms and the family now occupied the first one, which had a fireplace. Nasama had moved almost all the pots and other furniture not of immediate use into the other room, making the sick man's quarters more spacious and able to accommodate the people who came to see her ailing husband.

Musyani, who had never before been in Matenda's house, sat near the door in a manner suggesting that he did not plan on staying long. Again, he asked, "How

did *we* sleep last night?" but this time he asked more
softly, obviously so as not to disturb the bedridden
invalid. The doctor only burped in reply. Tepa, who
was sitting next to the doctor, winked at Sinka, who
sat farthest away, leaning against the wall.

"No sign of improvement," Sinka observed loudly.
"We had to send for the doctor earlier this morning."

There was a terrible smell in the room, a strange
and sickening stench. It was a smell of decay. Musyani
surveyed the room thoughtfully. There was a pot on the
fire. There was a bunch of roots lying on the floor
tied in six bundles, a basket of different kinds of leaves
and still another containing leaves that had been ground.
There was also a small pot holding a combination of
the ground leaves and roots soaked in water. There
were several bulblike roots and some of them emitted
a smell like that of onions.

Matenda was lying on a mat of reeds between Tepa,
his brother, and Sinka, his son. His body from the waist
down was covered with an old brown blanket. The
doctor had already taken off his two little horns, but
Musyani could still see blood clotted on one arm. On
the whole, he was surprised to see that Matenda looked
bigger now than before but it was not the sort of
bigness that suggested obesity. It seemed to him that
Matenda's body was swelling. Musyani could not see
his face because he was lying on his side with his
back turned, but once in a while he would hear him
take a long breath, then he would breathe quietly again,
so quietly that one would have thought he was not
breathing at all.

"And how are you yourself?" the doctor asked. "It
has been quite some time since we two met, hasn't it?"

The doctor sounded very friendly, Musyani thought,
not like the squirming creature who jumped up and

down on one leg at the beer feast, beating his chest and sighing. But could it be that Simbwindimbwi was only trying to put him at ease so he could attack him better when he was off guard, like a mamba which strikes without any warning when you are not looking at it? Guard your thoughts! Musyani thought. After all, doctors understand your thoughts just as easily as if you spoke them. He may know what I am thinking!

"Oh, I am still breathing," Musyani said, embarrassed. "I mean, so long as I can witness one more sunrise."

"Don't we all feel that way, though," the doctor sighed.

"That's why it's no use worrying about those who can get out and look at the sun," Musyani said. "They are living and they get out to look at the sun so they can assure themselves that they are really alive. It's those who cannot get out that we have to worry about." He was about to say, "those who are dying," but, thought better of it.

"In this era when witches have erupted like volcanoes," he continued, "all of us poor people who don't toy around with evil tools have been touched to some extent by them. They should consider themselves lucky who can even struggle to get out and take a look at the morning sun. Otherwise, we are all going to end up lying indoors like our friend here, too weak and in great misery, waiting for our end while the witches forage out and about, strong as rocks."

"I think we are disturbing him with this noise," Tepa said. "He seems restless again."

"Isn't it time for him to get his medicine?" Nasama asked. "He had his last dose before I went outside and it has been quite some time, really."

"I see the medicine has been thoroughly soaked," the doctor said as he peeped into a small dish which contained some leaves and a greenish-yellow solution with a pungent and peculiar smell. "Now," he said in a commanding voice, "make some porridge, using this water, and we shall give it to him to drink."

The pot on the fire had been put there for emergencies and it contained hot water at all times, day and night. Nasama put some millet flour in a dish and poured in a mixture of hot water from the pot on the fire and the greenish-yellow solution. She stirred this with a small piece of wood, and it was ready for the sick man to drink. This was the most difficult part because Matenda, like most people in his condition, did not like to drink his medicine. Sometimes he stubbornly refused to take it and threw it away in the presence of the doctor, saying that he would rather die than taste the "rotten stuff" again.

"You see," the doctor would say at such times, "it's the evil spirit in him that tells him not to take his medicine! No, he must have it . . ."

Tepa held the sick man's legs and Sinka held his arms, pressing them hard on the mat so he would not try to struggle free. Simbwindimbwi held open the sick man's mouth, and Nasama got ready to pour the medicine down his throat. Just as she was about to pour it into his mouth she faltered for some unknown reason, and the doctor asked Musyani by name if he would help the woman.

At the mere mention of Musyani's name, Matenda was seized with a most alarming paroxysm and shrieked out that Musyani was poking his chest with pins and needles.

"Take him away, please take his away," he cried

in anguish, kicking his feet like an animal that has just been shot. "He's tormenting me. Please take him away."

"Out!" Sinka ordered in a loud voice, his finger pointing to the door, his eyes glaring at Musyani with wrath. "Out, I say, and don't you ever come here again!"

Musyani jumped out of the house with sounds of "H'm!" "Oh!" and "Ach!" He had left his fez behind and was about to go back into the room to pick it up when it came flying out the door. He picked it up, wiped the dust off it and, putting it on his head, walked back to his own house. His eyes were red with anger and he beat his clenched hands against each other.

"By jove! It worked!" the doctor cried out, shutting his patient's mouth.

"What worked?" Sinka shouted back. He was breathing heavily, his body trembling and his face perspiring with anger. "What worked?"

"Why, this!" the doctor said. "I made this maneuver all on purpose. I made Nasama falter and lose her balance so that I could call Musyani by name under the pretence of asking him to help her. You see, the thing is this. Since Musyani came into this room we had never at any time referred to him by name and I reasoned that if I could call out his name at the time we were giving Matenda his medicine, the name would have a tremendous impact upon the evil spirit in our friend here. At the very sound of the name the spirit would collapse, thinking that its own master was betraying it by helping administer the medicine which is aimed at the destruction of the evil spirit. It was just that simple," he said, snapping his fingers. "Then, as soon as it collapsed there inside of him, Matenda might come to his senses and would thus be able to realize that it was Musyani who was tormenting and torturing him.

"He was talking here like he was innocent, saying, 'All of us poor people who don't toy around with evil tools . . .' Of course, Matenda heard every word of it, but to him the image of Musyani as his tormentor was being shielded, blanketed by the spirit. You follow me?"

"If Musyani doesn't unwitch him," Sinka swore, "I will club him to death. Just wait and see."

Matenda raised up and sat on the mat and presently began to vomit, spewing out things that were as yellow as the yolk of an egg. Tepa quickly brought a big white basin and placed it before him so he would not ruin the mat and the room. With his head bent and almost buried in the basin, Matenda continued to vomit.

"That's good," the doctor commented. "That's very good. It cleanses his insides. Keep on, Matenda . . . you are doing all right."

"Will the spirit come out too?" Tepa asked.

"Doubtful," the doctor said. "Keep on, Matenda . . ."

"You are all right, aren't you?" Sinka asked his mother, who, besides looking pale and obviously frightened, was crying.

"She will be all right in a moment," the doctor said.

"I will club him," Sinka declared again. "I will club him hard. He will cry and cry and cry and I will still club him until he unwitches my father, or he too must go if my father dies!" Sinka swung his hand and pointed to the door as if the dead expired by first going through the door and on to the outside world, inhabited only by those who must pass through the same door first. "You can bewitch a person too, can't you?"

"Me? No," the doctor replied as calmly and as

innocently as any angel. "My job is to cure illness, to expand life, not to terminate it. I know the various aspects of black magic that these demons use to kill others, but it is a necessity that I should know. I have to know them in order to be able to devise means of combating them and not for any other motive. That's what makes me a doctor, otherwise I would be just like anyone else here.

"I see that you are wondering in your mind whether I would, under certain circumstances, use my knowledge of the black magic for other purposes, such as bewitching someone in order to avenge myself and things like that.

"Well, the answer is no. You see, no sooner would I think of doing such a thing than I would immediately lose control over all the useful medicine that I now know. Not only that, but the same medicine would then revolt and kill me simply because I have betrayed it. The medicine, as you well know, functions best when there is a compensation of, say, a chicken or a goat or a cow or copper, just like anything else. You work harder when you know you are going to be paid for your labor and also when you are satisfied with the pay. It's the same thing with medicine. But it can never be compensated with human blood. That only makes it impotent and, with regard to its master, as deadly as a black mamba.

"In other words, you can either be a doctor or a witch or neither, but never both. The last is like bewitching yourself, and no soul in this whole world can cure you of that."

The doctor took time and the trouble to explain this, because he knew in his mind that Sinka was planning to repay Musyani—a tooth for a tooth and an eye for an eye—and that he was trying to solicit his aid.

"You should not think of clubbing Musyani or doing him any harm," the doctor advised. "The spirit will take that as an attack and it will then have an excuse for not getting out of your father."

They remained silent for several minutes. The doctor was sniffing his tobacco. Nasama went out to dispose of the porridge—now cold—that had been intended for Matenda's medicine and came back to sit near the door where Musyani had sat. Matenda had stopped vomiting but was still groaning. Precisely at the moment when Tepa was about to move the basin and the doctor was about to say something to the woman, Matenda was thrown into another fierce paroxysm, shouting and crying. He even stood up and attempted to run out of the house. Both Tepa and Sinka jumped on him and held him on the mat, where he continued to struggle and to kick his feet and wave his hands.

"Take them away! Leave me alone . . . Please, take them away . . ."

"Them!" Sinka gasped. "Them!"

"Take them away! Here they come, here they come . . . They are pointing quills at me . . . They are going to prick me . . ."

"How many do you see?" the doctor asked.

"Here they come. Please send them away. Please . . . Please! Please!" Matenda fell backward on the mat, made a long and deep heave, and after a short pause began to cry.

"How many are they?" the doctor repeated his question, but Matenda wept and said no more.

"Them!" Sinka was saying.

5

Late that afternoon Simbwindimbwi, with Tepa and Sinka, conferred privately with Mwenimuzi, the headman, in the latter's house. Earlier in the week it had been whispered throughout the village—and for no apparent reason as to why such a method of communication had been preferred—that the headman was contemplating a trip, the first in years. It was to take him to several surrounding villages, where he was to be hosted by his equals, spending a week at each one so that it would be more than a month before he showed himself again in his village. But Simbwindimbwi, after concluding that Matenda's illness, or "disease" as he preferred to call it, was such that it did not respond to any medicine and, like most of his colleagues, after predicting with "absolute certainty" that the ailing man was not likely to survive another week, sought to persuade the headman to postpone his trip. To be sure, he was encouraged in pursuing this line of action by Sinka's declared intent of clubbing Musyani to death in the event that his father died.

As rules of good etiquette dictated, Simbwindimbwi dispatched Tepa at once to the headman's house to inquire if he, the ruler of the village, had any spare time that afternoon to receive the doctor and his team on a matter of grave importance—"village emergency," as he put it.

"Why, it's an emergency," he told Tepa with great emphasis, as though the latter was unacquainted with the whole matter. "And don't you underestimate it in your report."

As soon as Tepa left for the headman's, Simbwindimbwi and Sinka stepped out of the house, each carrying a stool in his hand, and proceeded to sit on the veranda, their backs leaning against the orange-washed wall. A light cold wind was blowing down from the mountains. For some time they sat there without exchanging a word. Two women, walking in single file and carrying huge bundles of firewood, passed in front of them, each one saying, "Excuse me!" in turn.

Then Sinka said that nights were becoming cooler and Simbwindimbwi agreed with him, adding that he had hoped to patch his blanket that day, that he would soon go to Karopa, where a debt was owed him. He had one client in this village and another in that one who had not yet paid him. He said he planned surprise visits so that they would not run away, as happened previously when he announced his arrival. He would collect his debts and buy himself a new blanket.

"Lucky you," Sinka said. "I wish somebody owed me some money!"

At this point Tepa returned with the unwelcome news that the headman would not see the doctor.

"He won't see me?" Simbwindimbwi asked. "Did you tell him why I want to see him?"

"Yes, but he cut me short, saying he's very busy."

"Well, go back and tell him it's very important that I must see him."

Tepa was about to start back for the headman's house when the latter's messenger appeared in his official attire, consisting of a pair of brown khaki shorts without pockets, and a shirt and a red fez. The shorts were held tightly to his waist by means of a Boy Scout belt. The shirt, of the same material as the shorts, had no collar, but there were two pockets on which was painted in black the letter "A." The shirt, whose sleeves were as long and as wide as those of a jacket, was buttoned all the way up to the messenger's gullet with big metal buttons that gave the impression of having been polished only recently. The red fez had black tassels, and black puttees were wrapped around his legs.

The messenger walked slowly and gracefully, his chin up, swinging his arms shoulder high. When he came to the three men he made a sudden halt, stamping his gigantic bare foot on the ground mercilessly and making a salute with his right hand in a military fashion. Then he announced in a modulated baritone voice, "Mwenimuzi will see you!" Saying this, he swung his hand down sharply, made another bang on the ground with the same gigantic foot, and, after executing such a fancy turn as no one had ever before seen him execute, he marched back to Mwenimuzi, ruler of the village, shouting as he marched, "Left! Right! . . ."

"Let's go!" Simbwindimbwi said.

"I think one of us should stay here just in case," Sinka said.

"No, let's all go," Simbwindimbwi insisted. "We won't be long there."

Meanwhile the messenger had disappeared behind

the multitude of houses. They could still hear his marching monologue of "Left! Right!"

All the houses in the village were bungalows with grass-thatched roofs and verandas raised a foot or so above the ground. On these verandas the women sat in the evenings and whispered in one another's ears such stories and rumors as originated with them, and they whispered them with gusto. "She meets him in the forest!" "That rogue!"

However, when it came to size, the houses certainly differed. Some were bigger and taller than the others and in both these respects Mwenimuzi's was unsurpassed. He was the headman or "captain," as he variously called himself, and therefore he merited the biggest house in the village, where he could entertain official guests, which usually meant his nephews, inlaws, and friends.

As to the actual building of his house, he had done nothing but supervise. He had a method for getting things done. This or that person had committed such and such a crime at such and such a time and place and must be punished for it. This person had, to use his legal term, "entered into" the wife of another or—if it was a woman—the husband of another, and must be punished for it. Lately he had introduced the title of "your honor" into the general language, and so this or that person who failed to bow before him or had not said, "Your honor!" must be punished. All these people had been collected, judged, and sentenced to building Mwenimuzi's house. If a man had committed the crime or offense, his wife or one of his wives was also punished. If a woman were the culprit her husband too was punished. And so the criminals, as he freely called them, built him a bungalow with five rooms, and the females were given an added task of making pots for Mwenimuzi's wife.

While the erring ones were engaged in building the house and making pots, Mwenimuzi and his queen, a short fat woman with an uncouth countenance and a peculiar resemblance to a drone rather than a queen bee, would sit on stools out in the yard—sometimes they would sit together on one stool—showing each other how to string beads, as if this were a complicated matter. Or Mwenimuzi would demonstrate to his queen his ability to write, and at such times he would, with his forefinger, carve on the ground big letters, some of them with sharp corners and others so strange they had never before been seen in any alphabet, not even the Arabic one! Strange were the letters he carved, and he would take hold of his queen's finger and gently direct it over the big letters to the accompaniment of such exclamations as "Like that!" "That's right!" but just as instantly he would turn to his builders and shout, "Work, you swine! This will teach you!"

The men cut wood in the forest and the women carried it home on their heads. The men built the house and the women plastered it with mud. The women collected grass and the men thatched the roof. Finally the women whitewashed the house in and out while the queen shifted her weight up and down, burping and saying, "What a bunch of lazy women these are!" As a final touch the women stacked all the pots in one room where they carefully lined them up in four rows.

Mwenimuzi's messenger, who had already reached the house and who had been standing outside waiting for the arrival of Simbwindimbwi, Sinka, and Tepa, led them, as soon as they arrived, into the house, where they found Mwenimuzi sitting on an old chair with the tail of his satin robes resting on the floor. A silver chain, to which was attached a knot as big and as

red as a tomato, hung loosely about his neck. One of
his hands with its big white ivory bracelet, now yellowing with age, on his thigh. He had his eyes fixed on the
wall before him and he struck the newcomers as being
in a rather pensive mood.

"I have brought them, your honor," the messenger
said in his modulated baritone voice. "Here they are."
He made a long bow as he said this, then winked at the
others, motioning them to do likewise.

"Please do sit down," Mwenimuzi requested, pointing
to a mat that had been placed along the wall for the use
of visitors. The three men made their bows in turn and
proceeded to sit down while the messenger remained at
attention with his back against the door.

"I don't have time to listen to all the details," Mwenimuzi said. "Will you try to be precise?"

"Yes, your honor," Simbwindimbwi said. He had always considered himself to be as powerful or as important as Mwenimuzi himself and it invariably irritated
him each time he had to address the other as "your
honor," especially when the latter insisted upon it.

"Yes, your honor, I will be precise."

In the meantime the queen appeared at the door,
where she stood for a moment. Surmising correctly that
her king was engaged in some important business and
that her presence might not be appreciated, she disappeared, but only after she had told the messenger, who
was still standing at attention, where she would be in
the event that Mwenimuzi desired her presence.

"Musyani was here awhile back," Mwenimuzi said.
"He came to get my permission to go to the Boma tomorrow to see the District Commissioner. He complains
that you have insulted him and he wants to bring the
matter to the attention of the central government."

Sinka stood up to protest, but Mwenimuzi cut him

short, saying that he wanted to speak with Simbwindimbwi privately. If there was any need of the other two
men, he added, he would send for them. Tepa stood up
to join Sinka, who was already standing, and after
making long bows in turn as they had done when enter-
ing the house, they stepped out and went to Matenda's
house.

"What did you want to see me for?" Mwenimuzi
asked.

"About Matenda and Musyani," Simbwindimbwi replied. He felt very uneasy, recalling that he had never
before had a private conference with the village headman. What was this talk about the District Commissioner and the central government? he thought to himself. He took out his tobacco bag and took a deep
sniff. Immediately tears clear as silver glittered in his
eyes and he rubbed his nose in quick successive darts.
For some reason he felt a sudden noose of anger coiling inside him and he burped, a move that was regarded as an instinct in his profession. He saw something peculiar in the profound mood of the village headman, a mood almost verging on resignation, a mood
projecting the impression of genuine disinterest in a
matter that would have propelled his predecessors into
taking an immediate action. Mwenimuzi, with compressed and resolute mouth, continued to stare at the
wall and seemed to be carried away by some secret
thoughts.

"I don't want any trouble here," the headman said
without making even a slightest stir.

"That's it, sir," Simbwindimbwi said and instantly
put his tobacco bag back into his pocket. "We don't
want any trouble and that's precisely the reason why I
sought to see you. As you may know, Matenda is not
likely to live for another week and I am asking if you

will remain in the village until we see how things are going to fare."

"I don't want any trouble here," Mwenimuzi repeated with great emphasis this time. "Musyani is determined to go to Boma tomorrow and you know what that means, don't you?"

Simbwindimbwi, uncertain as to what the village headman was driving at, remained silent. He threw back his shoulders and continued to smile vaguely but he did not have the vaguest notion about the implications of the Boma and its law, whatever that was. Since when, he asked himself, did Mwenimuzi concern himself with such matters?

In the meantime Mwenimuzi noticed the messenger standing at attention and, lifting his braceleted hand, pointed to the door, motioning the messenger to step out. The latter, after making an exaggerated salute instead of the usual long low bow, stepped out of the room gracefully. Once outside he actually shouted to himself in a grave and ceremonious pitch, "Dismissed!" and walked casually to his barn, where, still wearing his uniform, he attended to the milking of his cow.

"You are afraid," Mwenimuzi began. "You are afraid that Sinka is going to kill Musyani, aren't you?"

Simbwindimbwi stiffened and felt a slight twitch at the corners of his mouth.

"Something like that, sir," he said and maintained his vague smile. Once again he felt very uncomfortable and his nervousness showed itself in his restlessness as his hand would now reach for his tobacco bag only to be withdrawn without it.

"Because he has bewitched his father," Simbwindimbwi replied. "That's why. And if Musyani should fail to release him wouldn't it be only fair to hold him responsible?"

"Musyani bewitched Matenda? Who says so?"

"Sir?" Simbwindimbwi shouted, obviously taken aback. He took a long, examining look at Mwenimuzi. Did the village headman doubt his authority, his supreme position in medicine? he asked himself. Finally he concluded that he now understood the other's concern about the Boma and the law. A wicked lie, he summed it up, and after convincing himself of this he concluded that Mwenimuzi had actually encouraged Musyani to go to the Boma as an excuse for getting Simbwindimbwi out of the village. Mwenimuzi, he decided, had come to resent him because—according to his own impression of himself—he was a man of grave importance.

Simbwindimbwi was elated with the notion of his own importance and even produced another vague smile followed by a profound expression and a compressed mouth. He reached for his bag again, poured a large quantity of tobacco on his open palm but suddenly changed his mind and poured it all back into the bag, which he continued to hold in his left hand. He heaved a deep sigh, and with his head bent forward, issued a short burp which sounded artificial even to his own ears. Then, bracing himself as though getting ready to engage in a duel, he said in a very challenging tone, "I say so!" Mwenimuzi's face showed a slight frowning gesture at Simbwindimbwi's challenging remark, indicating that he half-expected it, but he remained calm otherwise and as silent as a post.

"You remember, sir," Simbwindimbwi continued in a more subdued tone, "that you almost died a few years ago. We can only be thankful that we were able to discover the witch in time . . ."

"Oh, yes. I almost died, didn't I?" Mwenimuzi said lazily and with an air of indifference, but he now fixed the doctor with his piercing stare and seemed to be thinking, Who is "we?"

Contrary to what Simbwindimbwi was thinking, Mwenimuzi did not resent the doctor or his authority. The truth of the matter was that he thought him likable —queer but likable. However, he did not always accept Simbwindimbwi's pronouncements and lately he had become skeptical about almost everything. Even the doctor himself had said of him more than once, "I don't know what has entered into his head lately."

"I almost died," Mwenimuzi ruminated in the same lazy voice. "But coming back to the topic," he continued in a tone that was becoming more authoritative, "are you absolutely sure that Musyani bewitched Matenda?"

"It looks like I am on trial," Simbwindimbwi said, again assuming his vague smile and putting back into his pocket the tobacco bag. "I served our late and beloved village headman . . . that great man!" he said in a soft, sad, and singsong voice. "Believe me, he wouldn't even have thought of ever doubting my word. Never! He was a great man!"

"My father *was* a great man, wasn't he?" Mwenimuzi said. "I am not doubting your word, but do tell me how you have arrived at the conclusion that Musyani bewitched Matenda."

Simbwindimbwi laughed heartily, like a child, but observing the grave stare of the other, he stopped laughing instantly, mechanically, and put on a gloomy expression. "You know, sir," he said very seriously, "that we don't reveal our medicines!"

"I am not asking you to tell me your medicines," Mwenimuzi said gravely. "I am merely asking you to tell me how you have arrived at this conclusion."

"It's the same thing, sir," said the doctor. "It amounts to the same thing, whether I tell you how or give you all the secrets about my medicine. You can believe me."

"But Musyani denies any knowledge of it."

"Did you expect him to admit it?" Simbwindimbwi asked in a voice that suggested surprise at the other's apparent lack of understanding of the gravity of the whole issue.

Mwenimuzi appeared restless and irritated at what struck him as disrespect by the other, and frowned at him as if to reprimand him and imply, "That's not the way to speak to your superior!" He rose slowly from his seat, wrung his hands together vigorously as one does when one's hands are cold, and began to pace up and down the small room with the doctor's eyes following every step, turning when Mwenimuzi turned.

"I suppose you have already told Musyani personally about all this," he said, still pacing the floor at a deliberate and calculated rate. His robes almost swept the bare floor.

Simbwindimbwi shook his head but realizing that the headman was not looking at him and could not have noticed his headshake, he said in a low voice, "No, of course not."

"Don't you think you should?"

The doctor remained silent, but he too began to show increased signs of restlessness, his hand continuing to reach for his tobacco bag and then to put it back. He wanted to stand up, stuff his hands in the pockets of his satin shorts, and pace up and down like the village headman. But he neither stood up nor said anything. He did not even smile vaguely as he so often did. He fixed his gaze on the open door in front of him which led to the next room and occasionally stole glances at the pacing man.

"I know nothing about your profession," the village

headman said, "but I suggest that you should see Musyani face to face and tell him all about it."

"He would deny it, of course."

"Well, don't you have any evidence with which you
can convince him?"

"Evidence? Like what, sir?"

"You saw him bewitch Matenda, didn't you?"

"No."

"No?"

"No," Simbwindimbwi said in the same low and
tremulous voice, still maintaining his intent gaze on
the open door.

Mwenimuzi stopped his pacing, resumed his seat
with great care, arranging his robes with the same
care.

"You didn't see him do it," he said. "May I suppose
then that you heard about it from somebody else?"

"No."

"H'm! Then tell me the source of your information,"
he demanded angrily.

"I deduced it."

"Really, Simbwindimbwi?" Mwenimuzi said, spring-
ing to his feet and waving his braceleted arm as if to
say, "That is absolutely stupid!"

"This is really interesting," he continued, "and I
would like to hear more about it. If you will excuse
me for a moment . . ." He looked at the doctor and
without saying anything further stepped into the next
room and closed the door behind him.

Simbwindimbwi, now alone in the room and still
seated on the mat, was anything but motionless. He
thrust his massive fingers inside his shirt collar to
scratch his back, now rested his hands in his lap, now
laughed to himself aloud as though recalling something amusing. He sniffed some tobacco and licked

some of it with his tongue, successfully repressed a starting sneeze, and fixed his gaze intently on the closed door leading to the room into which Mwenimuzi had disappeared. All this time he wondered how long this would go on and why the village headman seemed to be in a bad humor, what fee he would ask for his attempts to save the life of Matenda, and if he succeeded in saving it, how popular he would become. "Famous!" he whispered to himself in a violent manner, at the same time jolting his body about excitedly.

Mwenimuzi! he thought with a proud and self-assuring smile on his face. Mwenimuzi! He will be ill one of these days, and I will see if he will still pace up and down like a king, screaming, "Really, now!" That will be the time!

A little girl came dashing into the room. She seemed surprised to find Simbwindimbwi there and, hesitating for a moment, sat down near the door and asked in a rapid and commanding voice, "Where is Mwenimuzi?"

Simbwindimbwi examined her carefully from his seat. "You are very disrespectful," he finally said with a serious expression on his face. "You just run into the room and shout, 'Where is Mwenimuzi?' Is that what your parents teach you?"

"My father sent me to find Mwenimuzi," she said like one who is determined. "Where is he?"

"My child!" Simbwindimbwi said, now moving closer to her. "That's not the way you talk to an important man. Your father is one of the most polite messengers that Mwenimuzi ever had, but you!"

"Where is Mwenimuzi?"

"I am not going to tell you if you talk like that," he told her, moving back to the spot on the mat where he had been sitting.

"I am here," said a big voice from the other room. "What is it?"

"My father says he will be in our house if you should need him," the child said and started to run out even before the voice from the other room said, "Tell him that I don't need him at this moment."

"Our children don't have any manners at all these day," Simbwindimbwi declared aloud but the voice from the other room did not answer him. "In the old days, one would have flogged her," Simbwindimbwi said in the same loud voice intending the village headman to hear. "But now they are being spoiled, and tomorrow they will be telling you that you are stupid."

Mwenimuzi's wife appeared at the door again, stood there for a moment and seemed annoyed at finding Simbwindimbwi still there. Struggling with the weight of her body, she squatted down near the doorpost and peeped into the room. "You are still here?" she said.

"Come inside," Simbwindimbwi said. "I have just been commenting on how rude and impolite our young ones are these days. In our day . . ."

"They are just children," the queen said, and excused herself again, remarking that she had an engagement at a friend's house.

The room was growing dark as the sun outside was about to set. There was a lowing of cows and the whistling of young boys as they called the cows by such exotic names as, "Mwakapitura, Mwambande, Mwakatundu . . ." A queue of chickens stood at the door waiting to go into the house to sleep, but they seemed unwilling to enter with Simbwindimbwi there and crowded themselves together at the door.

Simbwindimbwi wondered what was keeping Mwenimuzi so long in the other room when the other appeared at the door and without his usual robes. Instead, he was wearing a long-sleeved tunic, long khaki shorts and homemade sandals, and he looked very young. Simbwindimbwi rose from his seat and was about to arrange the chair for the headman when he saw, amazed and thunderstruck, Musyani trailing behind Mwenimuzi.

"Well!" he gasped, popeyed, clutching the chair.

"Thank you," Mwenimuzi said and proceeded to sit down in the chair, while Simbwindimbwi was still holding it.

"Now, if you two will sit down," said Mwenimuzi, "we will finish the matter."

Musyani, without uttering a word, immediately flung himself down on the mat, threw his back against the wall with a bang, and remained silent, his eyes wandering from one set of cobwebs to the other above his head.

"A trick? Well!" Simbwindimbwi was saying, still holding onto the chair.

"Will you sit down?" the village headman commanded.

Simbwindimbwi sat down at some distance from Musyani and never looked at him directly. With his eyes fixed on the village headman, he kept ejaculating, "Well!"

"Would you repeat what you were telling me before, for the benefit of Musyani?" Mwenimuzi asked, although he knew very well that Musyani, who had been hiding in the other room all the time he was interviewing the doctor, had understood everything.

"No," the doctor said rebelliously.

"Let's not be difficult," Mwenimuzi said, with a faint smile as though to imply, "Now, doctor, where is your strength?"

He repeated his question in a more serious and commanding tone when the doctor remained silent.

"No," the doctor said again.

"Tell me," the village headman said gravely. "Were you lying?"

"No."

"According to your deduction," the village headman said sarcastically, "do you still insist that Musyani bewitched Matenda?"

Simbwindimbwi remained silent, took a quick look of contempt at the two men, made another burp, and said in a loud voice as though he meant to surprise the others:

"I can't answer this. I am going out!" and he rose.

"Sit down!" ordered the village headman.

Slowly Simbwindimbwi sat down but he was determined not to answer any more questions.

"I am postponing my trip," Mwenimuzi said. "I am calling the council to a meeting on Monday and I want both of you to be present. You can now go."

Simbwindimbwi jumped up and headed toward Matenda's house, accusing Mwenimuzi of playing tricks and parting ways with tradition.

6

Sunday afternoon was very quiet and serene. The day itself was still and the immense sky, with the exception of a few clouds in strange geometrical formation hanging in one corner of it, was clear and blue. People had already returned from the church, where they always reminded themselves of their debt to Scotland and spoke of that country in terms as glorious as though Christ Himself lived there. And now, overcome by the immense heat, the men were resting on mats spread in the shade of the trees, some asleep and snoring loudly while others, still sitting, attended to the making of baskets and hoe handles and whistled odd tunes to themselves.

The women, as usual, went about their work. Some could be seen carrying bundles of firewood or big black pots of water dexterously balanced on their heads. Others were sweeping their houses or attending to various other chores peculiar to their sex. Matenda himself was still hallucinating in his house, kicking his legs, and making all kinds of demands on his attendants typical of people who know they are ill and want to remind everyone present of the fact.

A young boy came running along the street, displaying in his left hand a huge pheasant which he had caught in his trap in the dense forest on the side of the mountain. His mother, like most mothers who see emperors in their otherwise tiresome sons, jumped out of her house when she heard her son's voice and at the sight of the big bird in his hand she began dancing, telling the whole village that she had known he would bring home a pheasant. "Yes," she said, "he brings home mushrooms, honey, rabbits . . . My son! He's very industrious!"

Just at this moment a tall middle-aged man named Simeon with a catlike face advanced toward the middle of one of the streets, a short distance from one of Musyani's houses. Here he stopped and cleared his throat in a loud and rude manner. He was wearing a clean yellow shirt with red buttons, and a pair of long white trousers which were rolled up to his knees. A white bag on which were printed in heavy black the words THE WATCHTOWER hung loosely from his massive shoulders.

He remained silent for a few moments then began to speak, working himself up. Once in a while, after he had achieved a perpetual motion of swaying to and fro, he thumbed through the pages of the New Testament with his big and awkward fingers, always taking care to lick one of the fingers first. He stopped at a favorite page and read its contents in the same loud and forbidding voice. He pronounced each word distinctly; now raising his voice, now lowering it, now emphasizing a particular phrase with a violent wagging of his finger, then, closing the book he began to preach. He never seemed to care whether or not he had an audience nearby as long as he knew that there were people within hearing distance.

"Eternal fire!" he shouted as though he meant to terrify his listeners. He spoke more like a politician than a deacon and constantly pointed his finger at some imaginary hellfire. "Yes, my fathers and mothers. And you too my brothers and sisters. You will burn forever . . . You will ask for water to drink and Satan will give you boiling water. That's eternal fire . . ."

It was his habit to preach this message of doom every Sunday. He walked from one village to another, sometimes accompanied by his followers, sometimes alone, but always carrying his white bag in which he kept all kinds of pamphlets. Some of these, it was reported, came from as far away as New York and others from countries all over Europe and Asia. Some of them were written in languages he could not read. He received them all and distributed them to his listeners and followers, most of whom added them to their collection of paper to be used for rolling their cigarettes. If he located a pamphlet written in conventional languages and if his listeners could read, he would ask them to read aloud certain pages or chapters while he sat down to listen, every once in a while nodding his head and saying, "Amen!"

Neither the men under their shade trees nor the busy women running about seemed to be much bothered about Simeon's presence that afternoon. They accepted his exhortation as the occupation of a homeless man who earned his living by preaching the Holy Word from one place to another, year in and year out. Nevertheless, the preacher, undiscouraged, would look up to the high blue sky, and with arms outstretched, would cry, "God, All-loving Jehovah . . ." From time to time he changed his position to lessen the pain on his bare feet from the burning ground.

Presently the little boy who had been running in the street a few moments earlier, announcing to the rest of the villagers how he had killed a pheasant, came toward the preacher. He was wearing a small loincloth all in tatters and leaving bare his big navel, which seemed to be the most prominent feature of his whole body. He appeared bashful, dragging his feet. He knelt down a few feet in front of Simeon, took a quick worshiping look at the preacher.

"They sent me to tell you that you are disturbing Matenda," he reported in a trembling voice, then took off at full speed and quickly disappeared behind the row of houses, shouting, "I have told him!"

It was not until fifteen minutes later that Simeon decided to end his sermon, and even then the conclusion was reached only after an elderly woman had offered him a bowl of gruel. He preferred to consume this in the shade with the other men so he could continue to deliver his message.

Simeon carried the bowl with both hands as though it were priceless, walked slowly to the shade where he squatted down on the rough ground, refusing the invitation from one of the men to sit on the mat. Then he proceeded to drink his gruel.

"Aren't you ever tired of saying the same thing over and over?" asked one of the men in a toga that had once been a blanket. He had innumerable scars all over his legs. For some untold reason he was proud of his scars, describing them as the trademarks of a masculine man. "Only a real man," he always said, "would not be afraid of going into a thick and dark forest, feeling at home in its damp foliage . . . only a real man would kill a pig with a bare hand . . ."

"Tired?" said Simeon, wiping clean his thick brown

lips with the back of his palm, his morose face aglow. "How can you be tired of God, our All-loving Jehovah, our—"

"Christ Almighty," complained the man with the scars, "I didn't ask for a lecture. We are tired of hearing the same thing over every day. Why don't you tell us something new?"

Simeon emptied his bowl at a single gulp, licked his fingers with obvious enjoyment, and said: "My sermon is always new inasmuch as our All-loving Jehovah is always new." He let out a quick, loud, and satisfied laugh. After opening his bag he pulled out some pamphlets which he handed to the other with instructions to read them.

"Me? Read them?" said the man with the scars. "You must be kidding. I am, you might say, blind."

"Keep them in any case," said Simeon, and then began to summarize their contents verbally. He talked throughout the afternoon, loudly and excitedly, woke up those sleeping and made others discontinue their work, when he announced in the most serious tone yet that God's law absolutely prohibited any work on Sunday. Dinnertime came and found him still speaking. When the men gathered at the common eating-place from which only Simbwindimbwi, Sinka, Tepa, and the ailing Matenda were absent, Simeon was there pursuing his oratory.

"All the evildoers shall be punished," he announced in a happy manner as though he obviously excluded himself from the evildoers.

"They will," said the village headman with a smile, "but only after I have punished them myself."

Simeon was about to say something else when he was cut short by a command from the village headman. "No more of this preaching, Simeon."

7

A few broken white clouds piled up on the southern horizon and seemed immobile and permanent. An airplane had just zoomed across the sky and a high-pitched sound could be heard trailing after it. A slow and faint wind was blowing down from the mountain and it was noticeable only through the whisperlike whistling of the leaves in the tall treetops. Other than the broken clouds, the noise of a passing plane, and the light wind, it was a calm and clear night, with the full moon shining as brightly as if it were only a few miles away.

The village headman, wearing his butterfly-colored robes and homemade sandals, sat on a prominent stool in front of a glowing fire out in the open yard. Next to him sat Simeon with his white trousers still rolled up to his knees, his yellow shirt now unbuttoned, revealing his bushy chest. He sat with all the airs of self-confidence, his white bag lying beside him. The rest of the group was composed of a number of children, all of them squatting on the ground and listening with great patience to various tales that the village headman was recounting.

"The evening star," the village headman was saying, "is very selfish. It never feeds the moon. You can see for yourself how lean the moon becomes when it is new. The morning star on the other hand is very generous. It feeds the moon every day and you can see now how fat the moon is."

"But they are the same star," said one of the older boys on leave from school.

"You should all be like the morning star," the village headman said without paying any attention to the boy.

"But I want to be like the evening star," one of the smallest children said.

"No, my child," the village headman said. "That's bad. You should be like the morning one."

"But I don't want to," the child said in a threatening voice.

"Don't you worry," the boy just back from school said. "They are the same star."

"No, they aren't," the village headman contradicted. "They are different stars."

"No, they are the same star," said the boy with an air of intelligence and at the same time he grinned with pride.

"They are not different, eh?" the village headman asked, bending his head forward to take a closer look at the boy. "And who says so?"

"My teacher."

"And how does your teacher know they are not two different stars?" the headman inquired in a voice that showed some sign of annoyance.

"I don't know," the boy said. "How do you know they are different?"

"Back to your room!" shouted the headman, and the

other children jeered the boy as he disappeared into the darkness beyond the circle of the light from the glowing fire.

"What a rude child you are?" continued the head-man, his gaze fixed on the disappearing boy. "What are they teaching in schools nowadays? I should say nothing but rudeness and lies! You see now, Simeon, they make our children think they are more intelligent than their parents. I tell you, my friend"—Simeon let out a short and awkward laugh when the other referred to him as "my friend"—"we are just wasting our money paying fees for these rascals, a real waste of money," Mwenimuzi said angrily.

At the headman's request, one of the older boys put more wood on the fire, throwing sticks one by one carelessly into the fireplace while the village headman himself arranged his robes, an occupation that took a considerable amount of time. He then moved his stool farther back, with Simeon following suit as if involved in some sort of a ritual, and began narrating some of his own experiences as a young boy.

"This night," he started, "reminds me of the night many years ago when I was a small child just like you are now. Actually, I was a little bigger than you are.

"It was a chilly but calm and clear night, with the stars displaying all their brilliance. From the light on the top of the mountain over there we could tell that the moon was about to rise. We did not often sit around evening fires out in the open those days, so that most of the people were already indoors at that early hour of the night.

"I was sitting on the veranda of our house with my father, who was telling me about the day to come when I would become a chief, and how I was to discharge my duties.

"Suddenly in the darkness of the night we heard a multitude of footsteps and the sound of men talking in low voices. My father was about to stand up when we heard one of the men shout, 'We are not enemies. We are friends.'

" 'But who are you?' my father shouted back. They did not answer, but we could hear them talking to one another in the same low voices as they advanced to our house. Finally they came to a dead stop in front of us, a goodly number of them, both men and boys, including two Europeans who appeared exhausted, judging from the manner in which they breathed.

"My father, who was now advancing to the strangers, noticed that most of the men were carrying guns on their shoulders.

" 'You are not enemies?' he said. 'Why are you carrying guns?'

"Ignoring my father's extended hand, one of the men shouted in a rude voice, 'Where is the headman of this village?'

" 'I am here,' my father said, at the same time withdrawing his hand. 'What do you want?'

" 'All the men and boys in the village who are in good physical condition,' the stranger answered in a rude manner, like one who wants to impress one's authority on another.

" 'Who says so?' my father asked.

" 'The two Bwanas here say so,' the stranger said.

" 'This is my village,' my father said, 'and I suppose I am entitled to know why you want my people.'

" 'To fight Mlozi, that's why,' the stranger said. 'Now, would you gather your men together or shall I do that for you?'

" 'All my men are sick,' said my father. 'You will probably have better luck in the next village.'

" 'Rubbish,' retorted the stranger, and blew a whistle, whereupon the men with him started rushing into the houses as though they were policemen in search of criminals. They brought out with them all the men and boys that they found. There was a great uproar throughout the village that night as some women screamed in terror at the sight of these armed men, while others cursed them and called them thieves. My father told the man that I was sick, but he would not listen to him. They lined us up and gave some of us guns, while some of their force went to the barns to collect our cattle, including my father's favorite bull, which we called Njati because it looked like a buffalo. We were ordered to take the animals with us. Two other men ravaged through one house after another, collecting eggs for the two Europeans. We left that night, carrying guns and eggs and food and tending to the five cattle, leaving behind us a village of cursing women and children."

"Did you kill Mlozi?" one of the children asked impatiently while the headman began rearranging his robes and taking a sniff of tobacco, something that he seldom did.

"Just a moment," Mwenimuzi said. "As I was saying," he continued, "we left that night and walked all night long, and I remember seeing one of the Europeans shoot a leopard on the way. He ordered my father and three others to carry the beast because, as we learned the next day, he was going to skin it and keep the skin for medicine, I believe. The sound of the gun frightened the cattle. They started running away at full speed and we were ordered to pursue them. We deliberately ran slowly so that we were able to capture only three of them, letting the rest escape. We discovered a week later that these managed to find their way home.

Needless to say, my father was most displeased because his bull was among those captured. The stupid animal not only could not run fast, but when my father called it by its name "Njati!" in an attempt to frighten it away, it actually stopped and was captured. My father was very disappointed. He would have preferred to see the bull escape.

"Anyhow, we reached a camp early the following morning and found there some more men and boys and twelve other Europeans. Some of the men were being taught how to shoot guns while others were going through rigorous gymnastic exercises. We joined the two activities while the two Europeans slept to catch up on the sleep they had lost the night before.

"After our lessons, they had us kill one of the cattle. We also skinned the leopard, spreading the skin on the grass to dry and throwing away the rest. We roasted the beef there on an open fire and consumed some of it on the spot, carrying the rest with us to the next camp."

"Can you shoot a gun, now?" a child asked.

"Very well, indeed," the village headman said. "Anyway," he continued his story, telling it with great gusto, sometimes raising his voice and sometimes lowering it to emphasize some particular point. Simeon's eyes rose and fell, but he remained quiet. "Anyway, we left the camp that afternoon, tired and sleepy but with full stomachs. Besides the guns, most of the men were now carrying the meat, tents, boxes, chairs, and the gear, while six of us were given the task of pushing and pulling two cannons up and over and down the hills, and—"

"Cannons? What are cannons?" another child asked.

"Big guns," the village headman said. "We had to carry them whenever we were wading across rivers or streams. At the same time we had to look after the cattle, while the Europeans were setting the pace for us. I tell you, they may be lazy but they can walk quite fast!"

The headman asked another boy to get more firewood while he arranged his robes again and wiped his sandals with his open palm. The sandals were made of an old automobile tire and were as gray as the nails of his big toes. The nails, protruding out of the sandals, were themselves as thick as the bark of a tree. The boy, like the one before him, threw the wood on the fire carelessly, blew on it several times and soon the flames were leaping madly up and down.

Simeon, who had been quiet all this time, stifled two successive yawns within a period of a few minutes and tears rolled down his catlike face, but in order to assure the village headman that he was not losing interest in his story, he leaned forward toward the other and, displaying a pale and artificial smile, said in a polite voice, "Excuse me, Mwenimuzi, but are you talking about Mlozi, the man who used to live near the old Boma?"

"Yes, the very same man," the village headman said. "The same Mlozi. He was quite a man, wasn't he? He is the only man I know who brought terror to all the Europeans in the land. Every single one of them was afraid of him. That Mlozi—"

"H'm, I was just wondering if it was the same man," Simeon said, and then resumed his silence, sitting on the stool as motionless as if he were a wood carving.

"By sunset," the village headman continued his story, "we arrived at Mpata, a flat and very beautiful place with lovely shrubs dotted here and there, and short green grass on which we grazed the cattle that evening. It is really a meadow.

"Now, my children, when you grow up to be big

men and chance to travel there, you will find nothin
out of the ordinary. There is a small brook runnin
down into the meadow from a distant hill. The onl
thing peculiar about this brook is its water, which i
always boiling hot. The most startling thing is, of course
that there is another stream only a short distance awa
and, I believe, it also comes from the same hill. It
water is cold and clear as the morning dew.

"We camped in between the two streams, facing a
giant mountain to the east whose top on a clear da
shines like a mirror. It has many enormous rock
which, although precariously balanced, not even a
earthquake can put asunder. If you should ever scal
its height and reach the cool, windy top and look dow
below, you will see the great lake lying in all its majesty
its waters always on the move. On the far side of it
which is the end of the world, you will see immens
clouds, some dark, some white, and these join heave
and earth.

"They said that Mlozi and his men lived in a ver
thick and dark forest on the other side of the moun
tain. Few of us had ever seen the forest, but we al
knew the legend, common at the time, that befor
Mlozi and his men, no human being had ever entere
the forest and come out alive. It was reputed tha
ghosts lived there and that one could sometimes hea
them sing or mourn. That only goes to show that Mloz
must have been quite a man indeed actually to live i
there, sharing the place with creatures such as non
of us has ever seen.

"The plan, we were told, was simply that we wer
to climb the mountain the following afternoon an
ambush them at night."

The village headman paused so that he could atten
to his robes again and could ask the oldest boy to tak

the three youngest children to their rooms, as they were already sound asleep, promising the boy he would not continue the story until he came back. The boy, showing signs of fatigue, stood up and stretched out his long slender hands, then woke the children and escorted them to their room.

"And Mlozi, was he a Christian?" Simeon asked, leaning toward the village headman as was his habit when speaking to someone.

"No, he was an Arab slave-trader," said the other.

"He sold Christians, too?" Simeon asked, seeming appalled at the thought that anyone could sell Christians.

"He sold everyone," said the village headman.

There was a faint sound of drums from a faraway village, growing fainter as the whistle of the wind increased. The village headman said that people there were dancing to celebrate the full moon, as was their custom. He used to be a very good dancer in his boyhood days, he said, and wiggled his shoulders and his back unrhythmically to prove his point. Nobody, he declared, could ever outdance him in those days. "I was quick of limb and strong of body," he said.

Meanwhile the boy returned and resumed his seat. The village headman pointed his finger at another boy and said in a loud voice, "Your friend took the children to the house, now it's your turn to put some more wood on the fire."

While the boy was carefully and methodically laying the wood on the fire, the village headman cleared his throat and continued his tale.

"That evening one of the Europeans told my father to heat some water for the Europeans' baths.

"You knew my father, Simeon, and I am sure you will agree that he was not the sort of man to be ordered

around stupidly, not even by a European, especially
at a time when he, like every one of us, was tired and
sleepy. Well, my father turned to the European and
said, 'For goodness sake, why don't you go and bathe
in the brook? The water is already hot there.'

"The European, very much surprised at the answer,
stood stiff for a moment, with his gaze fixed on my
father. Then without uttering a single word he struck
my father on the face with his hand and shouted, 'I
say, heat the water.' My father's nose was bleeding
as he picked up a huge basin to go and draw water.

"All the men from our village had thrown away all
the guns and everything in the meantime and threatened
to return home that very moment because they regarded it as an insult that someone should strike their
chief so savagely. So we started to leave, all of us, including my father who had already dropped the basin,
but the Europeans and the men from other villages
attacked us, beat us as though we were children, and
tied our legs together so that we would not run away
in the dark.

"Early the following morning they untied us and gave
us some more lessons in the art of shooting guns. Also,
we slaughtered two bulls, including my father's. The
old man wept all day for his bull and even refused to
eat any meat that day. As he confessed later, he had
prayed all day that Mlozi would kill all those Europeans.

"We left the camp for the mountain early in the
afternoon and reached its bottom at sunset. We were
to stop there near a stream for several hours and
make a few rehearsals pertaining to the actual fighting,
which was to occur that night. The general procedure
was that we would climb the mountain at night, then
descend to the forest in which Mlozi and his men were

iving. We were to encircle the forest at once. This
lone, a whistle was to be blown and we were to shoot
ur way into the dark forest.

"We roasted some more meat and ate to the satis-
action of our bellies, with the exception of my father,
who was still brooding over the loss of his bull. We
began ascending the mountain in the early hours of
he evening, leaving the unslaughtered cattle unattended
behind us. Those pushing the cannons left first, fol-
owed by the rest of us and then the Europeans, who
ormed the rear.

"The moon had not yet risen, so it was not only
cold, but dark as well, although the night itself was
without a single cloud and the stars smiling at us and,
no doubt, at the forest sheltering Mlozi and his men.
We made our way slowly up to the top of the mountain,
jumping from one rock to another as though we were
mountain goats. Once at the top, we sat down to rest
or a short time, shivering with the cold breeze from
he lake, and moreover we had to observe absolute
silence lest our enemy should hear us and flee the
orest, which we could not see below us. One of the
Europeans pointed down the hill and said in a whisper
hat the forest was somewhere there and that we were
o break into two groups. One group, he said, was to go
o the right and the other to the left, each group plant-
ng a man at a distance of every fifty yards. The remaining two people, the leaders of the groups, would
meet at the other end of the forest and they would
blow the whistle, which meant action." Here the village
headman startled his audience with an emphasis on
he word "action," which he repeated to drive the
point across to them.

"Suddenly," he continued, "we heard the laughter
of hyenas far down the valley behind us, followed by

a great and confused noise from the cattle. They had been attacked by the hyenas, but there was nothing we could do.

"They put me in the same group with my father, and our leader was the same European who had struck my father the previous evening.

"We began our descent, the only sounds coming from rolling stones which had yielded to our weight and from owls hooting in the forest.

"Then the moon appeared on the far side of the lake, a brilliant glow upon the sky, a golden light upon the water. We now saw the forest for the first time and it looked fearful and imposing, but we were going to do our best. We continued our descent, guns on shoulders, one man carrying on his head the leopard skin, still damp and wet. The European would not leave it behind. The other men were carrying the cannons on their heads in order to avoid the noise that would occur by the squeaking of their wheels if they had to be pushed.

"Our leader turned around and said to me in a very low voice, 'Look after your idiotic father,' and ordered me to wait under a tree near a huge rock. My father was twenty yards away. As soon as he could, my father came and stood beside me, silently and anxiously. He was already perspiring.

"You must remember that neither of us had ever seen this man called Mlozi, but from the galloping rumors and the various versions of the legend that had come our way, we knew that he was some sort of superman, virtually invincible. People said he could fly like a bird, that he could turn himself into almost anything. A bird flew over and we stiffened, held back our breath. Had he, perchance, turned himself into bird? A stone rolled by and we were ready to scream

"We waited there for a considerable time, and every-thing was so still that we seemed to be the only people in that area. Indeed, we could hear waves hitting the shore far away down on the lake. The moon was quite high by then, and the gigantic forest lay ominously in front of us. Finally we slept, leaning against the tree, holding our guns.

"We jumped to our feet at the sound of a cannon, a sound so great that it must have terrified everyone who heard it. Then there was a great volley of guns, followed by shouts, as if from a hundred throats. Here we come, Mlozi . . . You are outnumbered, Mlozi . . .' "

"How did you know he was outnumbered?" Simeon asked.

"We didn't," the village headman answered. "At that moment we began advancing, side by side, and repeat-ing the shouts from the others, while shooting into the forest."

The children still present were beginning to show signs of impatience and anger at the endless tale of the village headman, and some were already dozing, others frequently yawning. One boy—highly pleased—was about to jump up and run to his family's house in response to his mother's call, but he was stopped by the headman, who answered the woman in the distance by shouting, "He'll be along shortly." The boy ground his teeth in anger.

The queen herself came over from Matenda's house, where she had been visiting and squatted down next to her husband, wiped the ashes off his yellowing bracelet with her palm, and said to him, "You seem to be enjoying yourself tonight, aren't you?" Simeon, who appeared sleepy and more bored than tired, sought to encourage the village headman into ending his story by commenting that Mlozi was not captured until several years later and at a place more than two hundred miles away from the scene that the village headman was describing.

"It's true," said the village headman, "that we did not capture Mlozi that night, but—"

"So, you didn't kill him!" complained one of the children.

"That's beside the point, my little one," the village headman said. "The fact was, of course, that Mlozi and his men had abandoned the forest more than a week before we got there, but we did not discover this until the morning following the night of our raid.

"Really, we wasted all our efforts to no purpose at all, except for the little consolation we had in the large number of animals we had killed in the course of our blind shooting, some of them mutilated beyond any recognition. Mlozi, if he had been there, would never have survived the fire from the cannons. That much I can assure you, although my father hoped that by his attributed qualities Mlozi would turn himself into a thunderbolt and strike the Europeans dead.

"I just said that we killed a number of animals, but a great many of them managed to escape, too. I remember very vividly one enormous animal—I believe it was a buffalo or some animal of that sort—charging at us from the forest, and the next thing I noticed was my father calling and shouting at me from the top of a tree, 'Come up quickly!' I didn't know the old man could climb so fast. I tried to be a hero and fired one shot but missed. I followed my father up the tree in the nick of time as the animal hit the tree with its head.

"We did not came down until the early hours of the morning, nor did we sleep up there. As we discovered later, most of us had either climbed or stayed there

about an hour after it started, since we did not get any
under the trees, as the actual shooting had ceased
response from Mlozi. The Europeans had spent the
night crowded together, with one cannon among them.

"We huddled together, one after another, summoned
by the piercing sounds of a whistle, all of us shivering
from the morning cold. A mammoth fire was built. We
were all counted and after finding that none was missing, the Europeans told us to roast some of the meat
from the animals we had shot. We chewed it ferociously
at that early hour of the day, the Europeans not excepted.

"It was not until shortly after sunrise that we gathered
sufficient courage to enter the forest and start an investigation. It was damp and dark inside, and we could
only grope our way around as we crisscrossed it,
crawling from one end to the other since one could
hardly stand up straight. The smell from the foliage
was dreadful, and sometimes we had to close our noses
and start breathing through our mouths. We crawled
under trees, our knees wet or bleeding, sending little
animals and birds fleeing before us.

"We saw no sign of Mlozi or any human being besides ourselves. I doubt even today whether Mlozi or
any man before us had ever entered that forest. I
doubt if any man would ever want to go there again.

"Finally, and after being quite exhausted, we came
across the spot where Mlozi and his men had been
living—a small cleared space on the edge of the forest.
It was surrounded by a fence of rocks, with a running
stream only a short distance away, part of which was
inside the stone wall. There were several fireplaces
and a number of discarded tin pots. There were also
some animal hides, which undoubtedly had been used
for mats. In one corner of the place there were several

chunks of dry meat lying about, and two elephant tusks which our Europeans decided to take home with them.

"All the things we saw at the site testified to the same thing, namely, that the place had been abandoned at least two weeks earlier. The Europeans were disappointed, but there was nothing else we could do, so we left the forest.

"We reached the place where we had left the cattle the previous evening only to find bones and a number of vultures perched on trees. We stayed there for the night, the Europeans in tents and the rest of us lying around a fire. The following morning, after serving the Europeans their breakfast, the guns were taken away from us and some of us were dismissed. The Europeans retained only a few men and boys, who were to carry the luggage back to their station.

"We literally ran home, singing and whistling, even my father, who appeared depressed and obviously sick but who still enjoyed rubbing his hands together and cursing the poor Europeans all the way home.

"Once home, we were given a hero's welcome as women ululated and touched off a general celebration of singing and dancing that lasted far into the night. But my father was never well again and he died only a few weeks later."

The messenger, complete in his official attire of khaki shorts and shirt, a red fez with its tassel hanging on the left, and black puttees wrapped around his staunch legs, was walking down the street in a rather exaggerated manner, like one accustomed to marching. He came to a sudden stop in front of a huge drum, which was tied against a tree near an anthill, wiped its surface with both hands, and, after picking up the two drumsticks which were lying on the ground, proceeded to give the drum a menacing beat. He was not only calling the entire village to attention but also reminding everyone that at the sound of a second bell they were to congregate forthwith at the usual meeting-place where they were to hear some serious pronouncements affecting the village life by Mwenimuzi himself.

He continued beating the drum, his right foot rising and falling with each beat, to the great amusement of the children, who had rushed out of their houses and were now surrounding him, shouting: "Harder, beat it harder . . ."

This accomplished, and with the forced assistance from some of the little boys who formed the admiring group, he proceeded to arrange a chair for the village

headman, who was to sit in front of his audience. He
instructed two boys to wipe the chair and blow away
whatever dust remained. Then he had them place some
stools. The first two rows were reserved for the queen,
the counselors, and the elderly men and women, leaving the whole empty area for the rest of the people,
who were to squat on the dusty ground unless they
remembered to bring their own stools.

After applying his final touches to the arrangement,
he stood straight, placed his hands on his hips, took a
long look at the entire set-up and, after fully satisfying
himself that everything was as it should be, dismissed
the little boys with a wave of his hand and marched
back to his house to wait.

This was in the early hours of the morning, and no
person, regardless of his status in the village, could leave
the area now that the first bell had been rung. This
took priority over all other things and the normal
course of life would resume only after the meeting.

The messenger gave the drum another beating four
hours after the first. This time he did not spend much
time on it, but no sooner had he started than the children surrounded him, asking if he would allow them
to beat the drum. Without paying any attention to
them, he continued beating, summoning everyone to
assemble together immediately, so that long before
he actually stopped beating the drum, people were
already flocking to the giant tree under whose shadow
all meetings took place. Mothers could be seen running,
leaving their crying children to trot behind them, while
the men pushed one another aside in an attempt to get
to the place before the Mwenimuzi himself.

The sun was already high and the day was growing
unbearably hot. For a moment, there was some confusion and shouts of "Look!" as an eagle swooped
down with terrifying speed and soared upward carrying

a rabbit in its beak. "Poor thing!" the people murmured.

With nothing to distract their attention, now that the eagle was gone, they made their way to the tree. Some of them had mud all over them, as they had just been plastering a house. The people of the village assembled below the tree, quietly and solemnly, as though they had just been told of some monstrous calamity. Those with advance information of the village headman's message were already starting to whisper it to their friends, hoping to elevate their own social status in the process. Nasama and a number of other women were missing from the meeting, as they had already obtained permission from the village headman to remain at home and attend the bedridden Matenda. He was now only a skeleton of a man—he had seemed much bigger to Musyani only a few days earlier—and Simbwindimbwi had declared early that morning that he was "very seriously ill."

They all sat down and made themselves as comfortable as possible. The older ones and such people as counted in the village or, as they themselves put it, the "people with shadows," sat on the stools provided, waiting for the village headman. He appeared shortly, walking elegantly in his black robes, which resembled an academic gown with gold embroidery on the front, a huge white helmet on his head, his sandals, badly made, on his feet, his white bracelet still on his arm. This time he was wearing his old pair of spectacles, which hung impeccably over his nose. He seldom wore these except on important or ceremonial occasions. He was preceded by his messenger, who carried a big dish and walked slowly, minding each step and setting the pace for the others. Immediately behind the village headman walked the queen herself, pushing her weight along and smiling at the people who had turned their eyes upon them. With her attention fixed on the audience, she found herself walking out of step with everyone else but she continued smiling at everyone. Then came Musyani and Simbwindimbwi, the one carrying a black pigeon in his hand and the other a white one. Both of them walked with their heads bowed as though in a funeral procession. They were followed by Sinka and Tepa, the only people in the group who marched side by side and seemed obviously elated at the attention they were drawing from the crowd.

"Stand up!" the messenger announced in a high and commanding voice. "Arise, everybody!"

Everyone rose in silence while Simeon managed to whisper into the ear of an old woman on his right that the whole thing reminded him of the Judgment Day to come. The old woman dismissed the remark with a shrug of her shoulders as the messenger and the rest of the group walked by in a slow march.

Once they arrived at the front row, the queen and the four men behind her stopped and stood behind the stools while the village headman and the messenger went straight to the big chair. The headman turned abruptly, the tail of his robes flying high behind him, and hurriedly seated himself on the chair while the messenger, now standing beside the chair, still holding the dish with both hands as though it were something precious, cleared his throat to say, "You may be seated now!"

As soon as the assemblage was seated, the messenger walked to the tree itself and placed the dish beside it, taking great care it did not topple. He then hurried back to the chair where he suddenly halted and stood at attention for the rest of the meeting, straight and tall and still as a statue.

The village headman rose lazily, took off his spectacles and held them in one hand while he thoughtfully surveyed his audience. He was about to say something when he saw Simeon waving his hand in the air like a child.

"What is it?" asked the headman with a serious expression, putting his spectacles back on.

Everyone stared at Simeon, who now stood up.

"I was wondering," Simeon said, "if we could open the meeting with a prayer, sir."

The crowd stirred and there was a general murmur of, "He's an idiot," to which Simeon made an unashamed loud rejoinder, "I am not!"

"Sit down," the village headman said in a serious tone, his voice revealing signs of anger. "One more such remark from you and you can be sure that I will send you away."

Simeon hesitated a moment, as if trying to decide whether to sit down or to leave the meeting, but finally he sat down and the old woman on his right took a long look at him. Their eyes met and she shook her head as if to insinuate that he was mad, but he only smiled at her. He was about to say something to her when she turned her head away from him.

"Our fathers and forefathers sat under this tree on various occasions and for various reasons," Mwenimuzi began, sounding more like a politician or a preacher than a chief. "May they help us.

"You all know," he continued, "why I have summoned you here this afternoon and I am not going to detain you any longer than need be by reminding you that it has always been the tradition of a chief to assure, at any cost, the security and well-being of his people. After all, what is a chief without people?"

One man whispered to another, "I told you he is a good man."

"Oh yes, he is a good man all right," the other whispered back, "as long as you don't forget to address him as 'your honor'!"

"Our forefathers," the village headman continued, "never took the life of a man without reason. If a man was a witch they killed him, but only after they had proved him to be a witch. If one man murdered another, they killed him too, but again only after they had proved the case.

"You all know that our friend Matenda is not here with us at this particular moment. He is ill, seriously ill, and it is in connection with his illness that I have summoned you here. A murder must be detested and abhorred. A witch no less.

"All of you or most of you, at any rate, have certainly picked up the rumor to the effect that we have within our walls a witch who is the tormentor of our friend Matenda. As will be evident very shortly, this is not entirely a rumor. It has some respectable foundation and I can assure you, my people, that this is precisely why I have called you today—to prove to you publicly whether or not such a witch does indeed exist in our village, casting spells and keeping other people in great misery. If this is true, it will only be natural that we treat the witch in accordance with our most ancient custom. If false, I shall ask every one of you to apologize to the man soon to be named for all the inconvenience to which he has unjustly been subjected."

At this point the chief paused to take off his spectacles and to hold them in his hand. Simbwindimbwi, apparently flattered by the village headman's reference to the "respectable foundation," kept his eyes modestly cast down on the bare ground, a faint smile glowing on his face while Musyani, who gave the impression of being preoccupied with profound thoughts, sat uneasily on the stool and seemed ready to interrupt the speaker

at any moment. He considered suggesting the possibility that there might not be such a thing as "proof"
in a case like this one. How would they prove it? he
was thinking. However, he remained silent all the time.

"Simbwindimbwi," the village headman called in a
sudden and startling voice, "did Musyani bewitch Matenda?"

Simbwindimbwi rose, still holding on to his pigeon,
and gave one of his vague smiles. "I have already expressed my views on that, sir."

"I want yes or no," the village headman said angrily,
again putting back his spectacles and swinging back the
sleeves of his robes. "Did he or did he not bewitch
Matenda? Answer yes or no, as the case may be."

"Well, sir," Simbwindimbwi said, "he did, so I
would say yes."

"Terrible," a voice from the crowd shouted. Musyani remained calm, although his first wife sprang to
her feet to protest. She had to be held to the ground by
the two men next to her, at the request of the village
headman.

"Musyani," he said, "did you bewitch Matenda? Yes
or no please."

Musyani rose and gave a quick and emphatic "No,
sir."

"He's lying!" Sinka screamed at the top of his voice,
but he was quickly reprimanded as Musyani's wife had
been. Simbwindimbwi, now seated, gave a long and
deliberate burp but otherwise remained calm.

"This is what I feared would happen," the village
headman said in a low voice, "and there is nothing
much that we can do with a case like this one except to
abide by the many examples left to us by antiquity.

"Our forefathers, right under this tree—if this tree
could talk, it would tell us a great many secrets of their
wisdom—were faced with innumerable cases similar to

this one where one person, sometimes out of jealousy and sometimes out of good faith, accused another of some guilty action. For the security and well-being of their village and the people, our great forefathers had to make up their minds one way or the other, always taking care that no one person was unjustly accused. We are called upon to do the same.

"You all know that an innocent person has nothing to fear in this world, for even a hungry lion will not assail him. It is no wonder then that our great-grand-fathers quickly discovered that even the deadly mwavi will not kill an innocent person if, for the purposes of establishing his innocence, he has been forced to eat a piece of root or bark or a leaf of the mwavi or has drunk any liquid into which any part of the mwavi has been cast by his assailants.

"I realize, of course, that our present government, which neither understands nor appreciates our great tradition, has made it a crime to administer the mwavi to suspected people, but when the security and happiness of my people is threatened, I am willing to override the government's ruling and that is just what I am going to do this afternoon."

Everyone stared at him, hardly believing what he was saying, for it had been many years since the mwavi had been administered to a person in the village or anywhere else in the country. The government, considering it a form of poison, had made its use illegal and even to be in possession of it constituted a crime.

No one seemed more incredulous about the whole thing than Simeon, who had already pricked up his ears and had one corner of his mouth turned down. He listened and wondered whether it was he or the village headman who was really mad. One woman thought the village headman was very courageous and admired him for it, and to express her affection for his stand she rose to her feet and began dancing and ululating to the amazement of them all. "At last," she was repeating, "we have a brave chief, bravo!"

"If you will sit down," the village headman said, "I will continue with the business at hand. I know we are all anxious to see our friend Matenda recover, but we also do not want to hurt any person.

"As I was saying, whenever our great-grandfathers were faced with a case similar to this one, they did one of the two things.

"Either they forced the suspected person to drink water mixed with some mwavi roots, which had the disadvantage that the person never came out alive unless he was really innocent, or they put the roots in a bowl of boiling water and made him dip his hands into it. If he was guilty, he got blisters but did not die. I intend this afternoon to do something similar to the latter.

"Despite the government's ruling, it has, throughout the ages, been the tradition of a chief to keep some mwavi in his household at all times. I have in that dish beside the tree some water and two or three mwavi roots. I have two pigeons here, our sacred birds, which will represent Musyani and Simbwindimbwi respectively, and we shall have the birds drink the water instead of the men they represent.

"I will part with tradtion in one respect, and that is, I shall start with the accuser, the white pigeon, which will hereafter be known as Simbwindimbwi and then I shall proceed to the other, which shall now be called Musyani . . ."

Simbwindimbwi protested. Might not the experiment, he asked, fail simply because the village headman had not observed the protocol demanded by tradition, namely, that you start with the accused?

"We shall soon find that out," the village headman said, and indicated to the messenger to bring the dish and at the same time he asked Simbwindimbwi to hand him the pigeon. For the first time, the bird looked frightened but, hard as it tried, it could not flee the firm grip of the village headman's massive hand.

The messenger stood before Mwenimuzi, holding the dish with its mwavi water, colored yellow by the small roots of the deadly tree. Even the messenger looked frightened, afraid that he was taking part in something that was illegal, but he remained faithful to his duty. The village headman asked for two men from the audience to come and help in the ritual, which only a few in the audience could remember even vaguely.

"May all the mountains, all the rivers," the village headman began reciting the formula, "all the trees and all the spirits of our great and wise ancestors help us.

"This bird is now Simbwindimbwi and has accused Musyani of bewitching Matenda. I am going to give him a drink of this water, and if his accusations are true, may he fly away in peace. If they are not true, I implore you, great mountains, wide rivers, and all you mighty trees and spirits to vindicate the innocent, and may the accuser never leave this place but dead."

Simbwindimbwi felt cold and he stiffened. He smiled confidently but deep down inside he was raging with fear, and at one point, feeling that he was shaking with terror, he stretched out his bare legs and set everyone laughing with a half-burp that accompanied the stretching of his legs. Musyani remained serious, his mouth compressed resolutely and his gaze fixed intently on the village headman and the other men. Unlike Simbwindimbwi, he experienced a tingling heat all over his body and he felt that he was about to start sweating, but nothing of the sort happened.

When it occurred to the headman that the pigeon would not drink of the water on his own accord, one of the two helping men was ordered to open the bird's mouth while the messenger poured mwavi water into it, taking care he did not spill it on the ground. This the helper did with immense success and sighed with relief and satisfaction as he withdrew the dish and put it down beside the tree.

The village headman released the pigeon and it flew away, flapping its little wings to the satisfaction of the crowd, as evidenced by shouts of "There!" issuing from many throats. The doctor stood up and, without wasting any time on burping, bellowed, "Do you believe me now?"

The village headman was about to say something before continuing the ritual. Many in the assemblage, having already concluded that the next pigeon would die, had started calling Musyani a witch. While the headman waited for them to quiet down, far in the distance they saw the pigeon losing strength and altitude. Before their eyes it began falling to the ground.

"Impossible," Simbwindimbwi cried and started to walk away. The village headman dispatched one of the villagers to bring back the pigeon. It was dead.

"Impossible, utterly impossible," Simbwindimbwi kept saying.

"I am afraid," the village headman announced, "that there is no point in going any further. We have proved our point."

Musyani jumped from his stool to meet his wives, who were already on their feet and dancing. Some people clapped their hands with joy while others took to jeering.

"I don't believe it, not a single word of it," Sinka shouted and walked away with Simbwindimbwi, followed shortly by Tepa, who was also expressing his own disbelief in his own manner.

"It's all a conspiracy," Simbwindimbwi said in a deadened voice. "They planned it that way. I know they did, and I can prove it," he kept saying, obviously justifying himself to the others.

Musyani released his pigeon, which had not been given the mwavi water. It flew away effortlessly. He watched it for several minutes and felt very proud of it. He even wished that he could fly so that he could follow it forever to the end of the world. Faster and faster the pigeon flew, smoothly and proudly, then it disappeared.

"There goes my innocence," Musyani said, pointing to the sky with a proud finger.

"I suppose you can go back to your house now, Musyani," the village headman said. "And may I be the first one to apologize?"

"And me too," added the fat queen, now standing beside her husband.

"I am going to sue them," Musyani said, and walked away in the company of Chande and Simeon, the latter declaring confidently that he had known all along that Musyani was innocent.

"No one would have believed me," he told Musyani. "Would you have believed me, Chande?"

"I don't know," Chande said.

"I suggest," said the village headman to his messenger, "that you bury this pigeon. Bury it deep so the dogs don't exhume it. It is poisoned. Also, pour the water into a hole somewhere, I should say in the latrine, and return the roots to my house as soon as you can. I don't think I need to remind you to wash your hands thoroughly."

"Yes, sir," the messenger said, made a salute, and proceeded to do as he was told while the village headman walked away the crowd dispersed. Some agreed with Simbwindimbwi that the whole thing had been a conspiracy and others said that no person on earth could play tricks with the mwavi.

9

Musyani retired to his first wife's house, where, for something like two hours, he played his malimba to the vocal accompaniment of both his wives and Simeon squatted on the bare floor with his bag resting on his lap, swaying to and fro as he sang. Mwenimuzi returned to his own house with his queen. Both of them sat on a mat was spread on the floor while the messenger stood at attention and received instructions from Mwenimuzi.

No sooner had the meeting under the giant tree ended than Simbwindimbwi announced he was leaving the village altogether that evening. With his eyes showing strain from both anger and sadness, his face crumpled, he remained in Matenda's house, collecting his belongings and throwing them carelessly into a cloth bag. He intended to leave nothing behind, not even medicine for the ailing man, so he threw the roots and wet leaves of his medicine along with shirts into the bag, paying no attention to Nasama's cries of protest.

"You are leaving us, Simbwindimbwi," Matenda himself said in a faint and almost inaudible voice. He was too weak to make a stir. "You are going . . ."

Simbwindimbwi did not answer but continued to col-

lect his things. When Nasama realized that Simbwindimbwi was serious, she too started grabbing at the
roots and leaves that were still lying about and hiding
them.

"They won't be of any use," Simbwindimbwi said
in a severe voice. "My medicine works only if it is
sanctioned by me, not when it is stolen."

"I am not stealing," Nasama shot back, throwing the
roots at him. "How dare you say that? We have been
feeding you, paying you, and now you say I am stealing
your medicine. H'm! Here are your roots!"

"Calm down," Sinka said to her. "Calm yourself
and behave!"

"Behave!" she said. "Is he behaving?"

In the meantime Simbwindimbwi stepped out of
the house, his bag in hand, and planted himself squarely
in the yard. His face was no longer crumpled but
severe and grave. He wore his cowbells around his
ankles and they produced a soft music on a slow and
measured beat as he took to dancing, jumping up and
down like a happy child, now on one foot and now on
the other. People gathered around him to hear him
denounce the village headman as an ignorant crook.
Simeon abandoned Musyani and his wives as soon as
he heard the general noise outside and came running,
his white bag over his shoulder.

"I am leaving," Simbwindimbwi declared. "I am
going home now, and let's see if your Mwenimuzi will
heal Matenda. We will see if he's both a village headman and a doctor . . ."

Sinka was already down on his knees begging Simbwindimbwi to change his mind, adding that he would
consider giving him two cows as a reward for his
services if he stayed to attend to Matenda.

"How can I stay?" Simbwindimbwi thundered.

"Didn't you hear the village headman imply that I am a fake, and you still ask me to stay here?"

Mwenimuzi himself approached, pounding his sandals on the ground, his spectacles in one hand, but he ignored the doctor and his audience as he walked into Matenda's house.

"You aren't a fake. I tell you, you aren't a fake," Sinka said, jumping to his feet and looking at the red sun, now slowly fading and about to disappear behind the mountain. "Is our Simbwindimbwi a fake?" he shouted to the crowd. "You are the judges. Tell me, is our Simbwindimbwi here a fake?"

"Be quiet!" the village headman ordered from the door of the sick man's house. "You are making too much noise for Matenda!"

Simbwindimbwi felt a twitch run through his whole body at the response the people gave Sinka. Happy tears were glistening in his eyes but determined to assure the gathering that he was not readily flattered one way or the other, he became even more forceful in his manner of speech.

"A fake! I have never been insulted so rudely," he declared in a loud voice, in defiance of the village headman's plea. "My colleagues would think twice before they called me that," he said, his face assuming a serious expression. He had stopped jumping up and down like a child. "But now," he continued in the same serious tone, "a layman calls me a fake! I am leaving—"

"*Are* you a fake?" Simeon demanded from the crowd.

The startled Simbwindimbwi stared at him for a few moments and then declared with ponderous gravity, "Certainly not!"

"Then don't run away!" Simeon shouted and started laughing.

"I am not running away," Simbwindimbwi said. "Who says I am running away? I am only resigning my duties in this village, because your village headman, an ignorant layman, has had the courage to insult me and my profession. I am going home—resigning, not running away," he went on excitedly.

"Are you leaving or staying?" the village headman inquired as he emerged from the house.

"Leaving," Simbwindimbwi said savagely.

"Then depart!" the village headman said angrily. "Go quietly and don't shout over it here."

"I am going," Simbwindimbwi said, "but, first of all, I want to tell my friends here that I am not running away. I want to tell them that you are expelling me from this village, because you don't like me, because you think I am a fake, because you—"

"Shut up!" Mwenimuzi screamed, and eveyone stiffened. "No more of that nonesense. Now, depart or be quiet!"

The red sun had already disappeared behind the mountains, leaving the night to be governed by the stars and the silvery moon. The moon was already creeping up over the farthest mountain. Little boys, whistling and chanting, were calling the cattle by name and driving them to the barns where the animals would continue chewing cud. Little girls, not wishing to be outdone by the boys, were also singing as they opened the doors of their houses to permit the chickens, standing in queues on the verandas, to retire from their scratching and sleep.

At the sunset hour of the evening there is always a gentle wind coming down from the mountain in that village, whistling and whispering so softly that you would think the mountain itself was breathing. But wait till midnight. The wind will have gathered momentum and it will no longer whistle but roar. The mountain will seem to have opened itself, sending out such merciless gusts of wind as to threaten the grass-thatched roofs on all the houses. The ghosts, they say, are then awake, are mobile, propelling themselves from one place to another by the might of the wind. It is advisable that the living remain indoors then, for the outside world no longer belongs to them but to the dead.

It is only a matter of time after sunset before the stars start smiling down at the earthbound villagers and beckoning them from their distant and sheltered positions. But they have been smiling and beckoning and laughing at poor men from time immemorial. Who in that village was prepared to appreciate them more today than yesterday? Matenda was groaning and dying in his house and the stars still smiled. The village headman and the doctor were wagging their fingers at each other and arguing just outside the house. The stars still laughed on.

If it had been one of those ordinary and happy evenings, the whole village would be gathering around several glowing fires, where the children count each star as it appears, giving it a name until such time as they can neither count all of them nor assign a name to each one because there are so many. Then the elders start imparting to the children their knowledge of the secrets of the universe as revealed to them by their great ancestors.

That evening Matenda was abandoned and left to listen to his own groans and moans while most of the villagers stood stiff and solemn around the village headman and Simbwindimbwi.

"Yes, I will leave," Simbwindimbwi said, "but in my own good time. I don't wish to be commanded."

At that moment Mwenimuzi dashed forward and grabbed the doctor's arm, shouting through clenched teeth, "Out! Away! Now!"

"This is ominous," Simeon said from among the crowd, shaking his head as he said it. "Whoever heard of a chief fighting with his men?"

"I don't want to fight," Simbwindimbwi said. "I don't want to be ordered around either." With a sarcastic grin on his face he added, "And will Mwenimuzi let go my arm?"

"Disgusting," the village headman muttered. "I will not let go your arm until you promise to leave this village immediately."

"Disgusting, indeed," Simbwindimbwi replied. "Is this the way a chief behaves in front of his people?"

Nasama, who had gone back into the house, now ran out screaming, announcing that Matenda had collapsed.

"He isn't breathing," she said between sobs.

"I am leaving," Simbwindimbwi said.

"No, you aren't," said the village headman.

"I say he isn't breathing, he's not groaning any more," Nasama sobbed. "Come in, he's not groaning!"

Both the village headman and Simbwindimbwi rushed into the house, followed shortly by Musyani and Simeon, Tepa, and Sinka. They sat around Matenda, who was still alive, although he was not groaning as the woman had reported. The village headman quickly excused himself, saying that he would return as soon as he could. Simbwindimbwi started untying his bundle, pulling out the roots and leaves from his bag and ordering Nasama to start preparing more medicine for Matenda.

10

Matenda died early one morning a few days later.

The sun had not yet risen but the signs of its coming could be seen above the treetops on the western mountain. The day's monotonous routine had already started. Young boys opened the barns and let out the cattle to forage in the woods. Others could be seen running around with big buckets in their hands preparing to milk the cows. The older women, who usually woke up before their daughters, let the chickens out of their houses and prepared to sweep the floors before inspection time. Inspection of houses was carried out daily by the headman's messenger and his team under specific instructions from Mwenimuzi, but it was never conducted at any fixed time.

Musyani was sitting on the veranda of his first wife's house in his usual attire of khaki shorts and shirt. He had been sharpening his axe and was now examining the sharpness of its blade. He was ready to dash into the forest, the man's world. The village headman, with a thick blue blanket wrapped around him in the manner of a toga, was sitting on a stool shaving out in the yard. Occasionally he paused to admire his face in the little mirror placed before him and standing on its own legs.

The queen, her contenance always more uncouth than usual at this early hour, stood in the door of her house, her hands folded over her chest, complaining that there was no water in the house, insisting that she was not in any mood to go to the well, because she still felt asleep. Would the village headman, she suggested, ask some woman of the village to do this favor for her? The chief did not answer her but continued shaving and humming an odd tune.

Then there was a sudden, long, and piercing female shriek from Matenda's house, followed by a chorus of several mixed voices. Mwenimuzi was the first to jump to his feet. Adjusting his toga, he ran into his house to get dressed, pushing aside the queen, who was still yawning and hanging lazily about the door. Musyani, who was still admiring the sharpness of his axe, hurried into his house to announce to his wife, who was still lying on the mat, that he was afraid Matenda had died. The woman let out a confused scream, rose to her feet nude and started searching around for her clothes. She was weeping all the time and saying how marvelous Matenda had been.

Musyani threw the axe into a dark corner and stepped out. He then ran to the village headman's house.

"What shall we do now?" he asked Mwenimuzi.

"What do you mean, 'What shall we do?' " replied the headman.

They exchanged a few more words while the village headman got dressed. The queen went on talking about washing her face and how there was no water in the house. As soon as Mwenimuzi was dressed, the two men walked to Matenda's house.

The messenger was already beating the traditional drum, summoning people from far and near. The drum communicated the information that the village had lost a man to death. People came flocking to Matenda's house. It soon became evident that the house was going to be too small for the immense crowd.

Musyani entered the room after the village headman. Both of them walked with their heads bowed, establishing the grave impression appropriate to the occasion. A stool was quickly brought by a young woman for the chief, and, wiping the tears off her face with one hand, she placed the stool against the wall with the other. The village headman sat down on the stool. Musyani squatted on the floor beside him. Both of them joined the crowd in the general sound of mourning. The females called out Matenda's name while the males chanted. Simbwindimbwi, also mourning and burping, held the widow's hand.

Matenda's body, all covered with an old blanket except for his face, lay on a mat surrounded by a ring of surviving relatives and the doctor. Musyani stole quick and broken glances at the dead man's face and thought he looked sad. Matenda's mouth was closed and dry. His eyes remained open and seemed to stare at Musyani in particular. Matenda has already found the answer to the perpetual question of what comes after death, Musyani thought.

"Don't be silly," Musyani told himself and continued to mourn for the one he now described audibly as "my good friend Matenda." The widow beat her head against the wall and Simbwindimbwi had to hold her down with all his force. Musyani jumped to his assistance. He returned a moment later to resume his seat beside the village headman, for Sinka was protesting, "Not you, murderer!" Musyani only shrugged his shoulders and continued to shed tears for "my good friend Matenda."

There was a terrible odor in the two windowless

rooms filled with people, partly from the mourning crowd, partly from the rotten and useless medicine in little pots, dishes, and calabashes lying about in the rooms, and partly from the dead man himself. The village headman, pretending to wipe away tears from his face, was actually holding his nose with his fingers. When he realized that he could do better by holding his breath at regular intervals and breathing through his mouth to avoid the smell, he changed his method. He discovered that this technique gave the impression of profound sadness as he held back his breath and then breathed out suddenly and loudly in the form of a deep sigh. To make the picture of grief complete, he shook his head while breathing out.

Simeon had arrived late so he could find space only on the veranda outside with the other latecomers.

"Did you know Matenda?" he asked the woman next to him, but the weeping woman did not answer him. Turning to a man behind him, he posed the same question.

"Did I know him?" the man repeated after Simeon, tears pouring down his face. "Well, I used to hunt with him," he remembered and broke into another frenzy of uncontrolled sobbing. His body shook as he recalled the incidents of long ago, which he had shared with Matenda. "We hunted together," he repeated between his sobs.

"Amen!" is all that Simeon could find to say. As if unaffected by the sorrow of the mourners, he pulled his New Testament from the white Watchtower bag which always hung over his shoulder and began reading to himself in a whisper. Now and then he called out loudly, "Amen!"

People from faraway villages began to arrive as the first rays of the morning sun struck out. They arrived in

groups of two or three or more, all of them following
the direction of the sound of the drum and the wailing of
the mourning people, as the Wise Men followed the star
to the city of Bethlehem. Men and women, the old and
the young, all came weeping and mourning even though
they did not have the slightest idea who the dead person
was. They knew all too well the essential heart of the
matter. Someone had died and preceded them to the
next world. Although they were lucky still to be around
to hear the drum and to mourn for the dead, there
would come a day when the drum would beat for
them. Others would come to mourn and the vicious
circle would roll on. Although one might accuse a
witch of killing one's own, they knew secretly that his
time had come. And theirs would come. So, the people
came, weeping at the sound of the drum, the same
drum that had, on other occasions, and with only a
slight change in its tone, made them cheer and dance.

The village headman stepped out of the room, partly
because he wanted to stretch himself and breathe some
cool, fresh air and partly because he felt obliged to
welcome the new arrivals, who had assembled outside.
He was followed shortly by Musyani, who came out
carrying Mwenimuzi's stool in one hand and rubbing
his eyes dry with the other. He put the stool in the
middle of the yard but the village headman preferred to
sit on the ground with the rest of the people. Simbwindimbwi, who looked tired and depressed and wore a
gloomy expression on his face as if he considered the
whole thing a personal loss, came out next. He went
straight to the village headman and whispered something into his ear.

"Yes, I think it's time we started building the house,"
the village headman answered in a low and subdued
voice. He meant that it was time they started digging

the grave. "We shall have to bury him this afternoon," he continued in the same melancholy voice.

Simbwindimbwi went back into the house and in spite of the deafening noise of the mourners was able to get the attention of the males. Repeating the village headman's words, he notified them that they must soon start building the house.

The men, other than Sinka and Tepa, took advantage of the announcement to flee immediately the pungent smell in the room. Their places were soon filled by women from outside. Once outside, the men sat on the ground to greet the people, just as the village headman had done before them. This enabled them to bring the visitors up-to-date about the dead person—the cause of his death, the gossip about Musyani, his family connections, and the like.

"I saw Matenda not too long ago," one of the new arrivals said. "A strong man he was then! Certainly," he went on, "he must have been bewitched!"

Also, the men caught up on their sniffing and smoking, whispering to one another and even laughing in low voices. The women indoors were, in the course of their weeping and singing, praising to the skies the kind of life that Matenda had led, so that even those who had never known the man were joining in the general praise of him.

"I say, let's get started," the village headman said with a wave of his arm, encircled by its huge white bracelet. "We would do well to have it finished before the sun gets too hot."

At this announcement everybody started for his respective house to fetch hoes and picks. They then filed to the graveyard, their equipment over their shoulders, and were joined by the village headman and the male visitors.

"Here," Mwenimuzi said. "We are going to build it here."

The site he selected was at the farther end of the graveyard, twenty feet beyond the nearest grave, on which stood a crudely made wooden cross that gave the impression of having been hastily put together. There were hundreds of graves, some with elaborate crosses and some without, and there were some that even had grass-thatched roofs over them supported by a number of pillars. On some of the graves were little pots and calabashes into which survivors put beer in order to earn some favors from their deceased relatives.

"Wait," the village headman said suddenly, his face raised to the sky in a mood of deep meditation. "I am just wondering whether anybody knows if any of Matenda's relatives are buried in this yard? We have to bury him beside his relatives, you know."

Apparently he decided that there was no relative of Matenda's buried in the graveyard, for he asked the men to start digging the grave at the site he had already selected.

For no particular reason, other than that he liked the idea, Simeon asked the village headman in a very serious tone if he could be the first one to break the ground, adding that he had never had that privilege before. After obtaining the chief's permission he picked up a hoe and started digging. A broad smile spread over his face. He stopped only once to roll up the sleeves of his yellow shirt. Several minutes later he threw down the hoe, saying that he had done his share of the job and that others should take over from there.

"If four more people would dig," he said, admiring his own work, "each doing as much as I have done, we could finish the grave in no time at all."

Two men began digging while the others sat down on the grass or on old graves. Without any consideration for the gravity of the situation, they began telling stories and cracking jokes and laughing as loudly as they pleased. The gravediggers stopped their work to laugh too. Only when forced to do so did they resume their digging. Both Musyani and Simbwindimbwi, at different times, did their share of grave-digging, each laughing under his breath whenever someone told an amusing joke. The village headman started one of his endless tales about how he used to dance during his boyhood days and how he and the other boys used to set up traps in the forests. He described these incidents with graphic vividness, obviously enjoying himself. The messenger, who sat a little way from the headman, with his fez on the back of his head and his hands fiddling with his Boy Scout belt, listened with great attention, nodding his head to suggest his absolute agreement with the other's tale. He knew nothing about what Mweni-muzi was talking about except that, as usual, he felt attention was part of his duty to the village headman.

Two men got up to relieve the others at the grave-digging. The grave was now more than four feet deep and nearing completion. The village headman rose, as the whole group burst into an uproar of laughter after one of his jokes, and walked to within two feet of the edge of the rectangular hole. After peering into it and commenting on the splendid progress of the job he returned to his seat to continue his tale.

"A pig," he was saying, his face all smiles. "I killed my first pig when I was only twelve. Isn't that something? Mind you," he continued, "I didn't catch it in a trap or shoot it. That's cheating. I speared it, all alone."

"But didn't you run away from a lion?" Simeon wanted to know, while everyone else braced their nerves, silently rebuking Simeon for being so daring as to ask the village headman such an embarrassing question.

"Well, I did," the village headman said, laughing. "But didn't I come back to kill the beast without anybody's assistance?"

"With the assistance of the gun," Simeon said.

"I'm not stupid," the village headman said angrily. One of the men motioned Simeon to discontinue the subject. "I wasn't going to attack the beast empty-handed, so I ran home to collect my gun."

By now the early hours of the afternoon had arrived and the sun in the cloudless sky was shining with all its power. The women in the funeral house had changed their weeping into a slow chanting and were singing funeral songs. The voice of the widow, at a very high pitch, could very easily be discerned above the multitude of female voices.

A general silence fell over the men at the grave, the sort of silence that often imposes itself on an audience, allowing an individual to be carried away into a world of his own and known to himself alone. Sweat dripped from the brows of the gravediggers and their bodies were smeared dark brown with dirt, their hearts pounding within as they stood back to examine their work.

The hole was now seven feet deep and they started carving a cave on one side. The village headman reminded them that the Musyani clan were always buried with their heads facing north so the gravediggers carved the cave on the north side of the hole, for the cave was to be the dead man's eternal bed.

"Does anyone know how tall Matenda is?" one of the gravediggers asked.

"I'll have someone go and measure him," the village headman said and dispatched his messenger, who returned shortly carrying a long reed with a mark on it.

"This tall," the messenger said, the reed pressed to his chest and his finger pointing at the mark on the reed.

One of the gravediggers took the reed and cut it at the mark and measured the length of the cave, whereupon he announced excitedly, "I think we're done!"

"Will three of you come along with me?" the village headman asked.

Three stout men, all wearing loincloths, rose simultaneously, and with the wave of his braceleted arm the village headman indicated to the messenger that he too was to come along.

The village headman licked his lips merrily, almost like a child, but he tightened them as he turned to survey the men who were to accompany him to the house. By the sudden seriousness on his face he meant to set an example for them to act accordingly. One of the men, a heavy-bearded fellow, wanted to know if they were going to carry Matenda's body.

"I am afraid, sir," he said, "I always have horrible nightmares whenever I see dead people," and he began pulling on his beard in embarrassment.

"You aren't carrying Matenda," said the village headman. "Let's go."

He led the way, followed by his messenger, with the three men at the rear. All of them walked slowly toward the house, their eyes cast down and their faces gloomy to suit the occasion. They now behaved more like men at a funeral and less like storytellers. They stopped in front of the headman's house while Mwenimuzi went inside to his storeroom. It was a small, dark room. Feeling his way about with his hands, he found a small suitcase, picked it up, and carried it to an adjacent room where there was light. He proceeded to open the worn-out box, now totally discolored by age. He took his time examining every little item in the box. There were ancient and rusty coins, various buttons, beads, pieces of hair from all sorts of animals, little pieces of horns and porcupine quills. He examined each item, then threw it back into the suitcase.

As though angry at not finding what he was looking for, he closed the suitcase carelessly and with a bang and took it back to the dark room. After spending some moments groping around, he reappeared, dragging a huge trunk behind him. He wiped the dust off the top quickly and opened it by pulling the latches. He pulled out a new white cloth, which he cut in two with a pair of scissors that he had fished out of a nearby pot. He put one piece of the cloth back into the trunk and closed the lid. Not bothering to drag the trunk back to the dark room, he emerged from the house with a piece of the cloth under his arm.

"I don't want to go into the house," the bearded fellow said when they reached Matenda's house. "As I said before, I will have nightmares for days on end if I should see him."

"All right," said the village headman. "Go back to the graveyard."

The man ran back, cheerful that a nightmare had been spared him, while the others entered the house to join the women. A stool was quickly produced for the village headman, who sat down on it immediately. The other men sat on the floor. After several minutes of complete silence, with his head buried between his knees, the headman raised his eyes and stared for a few moments at the uncovered face of the dead person. He wondered if he too was going to have nightmares. He dismissed the thought by reminding himself that he had seen many dead people in his life and one more would not make much difference.

"Pardon me," he said in a low voice, one intended to imply that it came from a sad heart. "Excuse me, the house is almost ready and would someone get the water ready?"

The women who had ceased weeping and singing to listen to him started again in low voices. Two women went out and returned with a big basin of water and placed it beside the dead Matenda. The men started washing him. Without waiting to dry his body they wrapped the white cloth the headman had brought around his head. The widow let out a piercing scream. This was the last time she would see her husband's face, she moaned. The men continued to cover his head and his face with the cloth. Methodically they wrapped the rest of his body, first in an old and dirty blanket and then in a mat only recently made.

The gravediggers had finished their job and had laid a number of small logs in the cave where Matenda was to rest. They were sitting down with the rest of the men, most of them lounging in the shade, talking and laughing merrily. Those inside the house had seen the last of Matenda, now only a bundle on the floor. The village headman turned to the messenger and, in a solemn voice, ordered him to beat the drum again.

Except for the funeral, the day was perfectly beautiful. Everything was still and calm. It was the sort of day one would like to wander in the forests, rub shoulders with bats or lie down under the trees and meditate or sleep; the sort of day when one feels happy for no reason except the thought of being alive and able to appreciate one's surroundings. The messenger stood outside, tall and firm, and forced tears out of his eyes as he suddenly remembered that only yesterday Matenda was just as alive as he was now. He looked at the sky and wondered why man was not as permanent as the sun itself, but, mindful of his duty, he picked up the drumsticks and started beating the drum.

The men at the grave rose in solemn silence at the first sound of the drum. The bearded fellow started to walk away and finally sat down behind an anthill, to hide himself from the dead. The village headman inside the house rose from his seat and stepped out. The two men bowed low, one after the other, and picked up the body of Matenda. They stepped out with their burden, followed by the whole multitude of mourning women. The widow was now being supported by her son, Sinka, and Tepa, her brother-in-law.

They walked in a slow procession, the village headman leading the way. The men at the grave started singing, imploring the deity to welcome the new arrival. They laid the body beside the grave while the village headman recited his brief eulogy, in which he told the ancestors about Matenda's career, ending with the note that the village was sad to part with him but, at the same time, happy that he was joining the wise ones.

At this point the men slowly lowered the body into the grave, carefully laid it on the logs in the cave and began putting the dirt back, filling in the hole, as Sinka and Tepa held the widow, Nasama, who was kicking her legs and screaming, "Put me there too."

The graveyard was richer by one as the new grave stood prominently, almost majestically, a foot above the ground. Matenda had joined the ranks of the dead and perhaps he too would start roaming the world at night when the wind roars and the living are asleep.

Simeon said the closing prayer at the request of the village headman. "Almighty Jehovah, we bequeath to you your servant Matenda . . ."

There was a moment of silence and then the crowd walked slowly away.

11

"Fire!" a woman screamed in the dark. "Fire!"

It was late at night and the people—except the children who were already asleep—were sitting around fires in front of the dead man's house. The sky was overcast and thick clouds could be seen floating over the mountain and blanketing the moon.

Suddenly the people saw huge flames shooting through the roof of the house of Musyani's first wife. There followed a moment of amazement and indecision as each one tried to make out what this could mean, but the fire flamed on, eating away the house and preparing to spread itself to the next house.

Women started screaming and running into their houses, from they emerged with big pots of water on their heads. They emptied them on the roof of the second house while men were pulling down the roof itself. In a few minutes Musyani's house was all burned down and with it everything he owned except two chickens which had managed to jump out of the house through the leaping flames. One of them died shortly afterward.

The village headman, who had been standing not far from the burning house, rubbing his hands together and biting his lips, ran back to the dead man's house. When he went into the house he found Sinka and Tepa sitting on opposite sides of the fireplace. He demanded, "Sinka! Tepa! Did you burn Musyani's house?"

There was no answer. Sinka started mourning, and Tepa followed suit.

"I am asking you a question. Did you burn the house?"

"What house, sir?" both of them asked sadly.

"What do you mean?" the village headman said in a menacing tone. "Just answer me, did you or didn't you burn the house?"

"No, sir," both of them said. "We didn't."

The second house had been saved, but it stood there with only a few rafters, as most of the structure had been pulled down along with the grass. Frightened women were ordering their children to stand far away from the first house, as pots and jars were exploding, sending flames high.

The village headman returned and called for Musyani, but there was no response. He altered all the men to look for him, but he was nowhere to be found. His wives, weeping over the loss of the house rather than Matenda, only shrugged their shoulders.

12

A narrow dusty road runs along the edge of the village from the old Boma, winding its way like a snake up the mountain. Once at the top of the mountain, a plateau-like area covering several square miles, the road assumes a straight course for three or four miles. It then begins to zigzag down to the valley in a score of breathtaking hairpin turns. When the road reaches the valley, it assumes a straight course once more, so straight that anthills and houses that lay in its path had to be demolished. When one stands on the edge of a mountaintop on a clear day and looks down at the valley and at the straight road growing narrow with the distance, burying itself under the magnificent tall trees at one point, reappearing at the next, and then disappearing altogether over the horizon, one is inevitably reminded of the straight and narrow path to the heavenly gate.

This particular road, all of it, is the masterpiece of the prisoners of the law who, with picks and hammers and hoes, carved it. An armed guard always accompanied them. With his gun over his shoulder, his head buried under a thick gray helmet, his whip in hand, he would trail behind them. He was free, almost generous with his whip, which, whenever the spirit moved him, he lifted methodically and with great zest, landing it on the bare back of a stooping prisoner and shouting to high heaven, "Work, you lazy swine!" He would then collect his salary at the end of the month. The prisoners built the road through thick and thin and now it stands as a positive reminder to all future generations of the power of the law.

No person uses this road as often as does a Catholic priest, Father Puccinni, a man with long golden hair, imposing temples and a prominent Adam's apple. Regardless of the weather, he wears a khaki robe and comes charging into the village on his ancient motorcycle, smoke and dust flying behind him.

He always stops in the village. Sometimes he stays for days on end. He dismounts from his machine and parks it in the yard and, opening the carriage in which he also stores his spare gasoline, he pulls out packets of candies and distributes these to the children, whom he knows by name. The children adore him. He always brings with him several packets of cigarettes which he opens. He gives one cigarette to each man. He sits down among them, always taking care to sit at a reasonable distance from the women. If the men are drinking, he joins them, talking to them in their own language. They praise him to the skies, saying that he is one of them. Sometimes, he takes one child after another on his motorcycle and drives around the village.

The children have memorized the sound of his machine so that even when he is miles away from the village they start jumping up and down in jubilation, calling one another and shouting, "He is coming, Father Puccinni is coming!" and they assemble at the end of the village to meet him.

Father Puccinni enjoys this sort of welcome. He always stops his machine when he sees them, and after greeting them he inquires how they have been behaving since he saw them last.

Father Puccinni came during the early hours of the morning following the day of Matenda's death. As usual the children gathered to meet him, but, attracted by the large crowd of people, he came straight to the dead man's house. At the sight of him the widow exaggerated her mourning. She was now sitting on the floor and resting her elbow on an old four-legged stool, a pair of red eyes bulging in her pale wan face and her breasts, which were left bare, drooping down lifelessly, reminding her that she was no longer a young girl.

"He died yesterday," she wept and called to Puccinni. "Your friend Matenda left us yesterday morning . . ."

All this time Puccinni was parking his motorcycle under a tree, an occupation that took him longer than usual. This accomplished, slowly he wiped the dust off his khaki robe and made the sign of the cross. Fiddling with his rosary, he perched on a mat spread on the veranda. He leaned forward to listen to a detailed account of Matenda's illness and death from the village headman himself, with frequent interruptions from Nasama, who kept repeating, "We buried him yesterday . . ."

Meanwhile, the children had gathered around the motorcycle. Sucking their thumbs, looking now at the machine and now at the owner, they implored him with their eyes to give them the candies which they knew he had brought for them. He was listening intently to the village headman and to the weeping of the widow. The latter affected him and, tears were soon glistening in the good priest's blue eyes.

"Terrible!" he said softly. "Terrible!" Once more

he made the sign of the cross, touched a few beads of his rosary, and then turned to console the woman.

A little child who could wait no longer advanced to the mat where he sat down and began stroking the priest's golden hair.

"Go back to your friends," the village headman said, but the child remained, stroking the priest's hair.

There was another sound in the distance, this time the sound of a car. Dust could be seen flying high in the morning air. Worried mothers gathered their children together and called to others to stay clear of the road. The drivers, especially Europeans, were notorious for driving at high speeds, blowing their horns as they went.

"The Police!" someone shouted as a purple Land-Rover appeared at the end of the village. "The Police are coming!" the same person shouted in a high-pitched voice as if he meant to frighten the rest of the villagers.

Simbwindimbwi emerged lazily from the house after hearing the first cry of "Police," and stood in the doorway for a few moments, like one who is trying to decide on something grave and urgent. He looked down at the priest and gave him a vague smile, then, without any warning, he shot off at a determined trot and disappeared behind the house.

The Land-Rover came to a dead stop in front of the house. Both the village headman and the priest were already on their feet as three black policemen jumped out of the car, followed shortly by Musyani himself.

"So you went to the Boma!" the village headman gasped, his eyes popping out. "We looked for you all over the village last night, but you had fled to the Boma, and without even notifying us!"

"Welcome!" Puccinni greeted, a happy smile on his childlike face.

Musyani smiled at the priest but the policemen ignored him as they adjusted their black caps, which, until then, had been resting at the back of their heads. They clicked together the heels of their black boots. Then their leader lit the cigarette which he had been holding in his hand and pulled out of his shirt pocket a blue piece of paper bearing some official markings. He unfolded this awkwardly and proceeded to read from it in a firm voice. He was an enormous man, heavily built, with a face that seemed to have been carved in a hurry. On it stood a huge and broad nose with two rolls of hair sticking out of the nostrils, a pair of brown, sunken eyes which had a frightful stare. He wore a tight-fitting pair of brown khaki shorts with black trimmings on the sides, a short-sleeved white shirt which differentiated him from the other two also told of his superiority over them.

"The village headman here?" he said in the same firm and powerful voice while his eyes scrutinized the smile on the priest's face.

"Yes, Bwana," the village headman said in a terrified voice. "I am here, sir," he continued, raising his right hand as if to indicate to the policeman where he was standing.

"Your name?"

"My name?" the startled village headman asked. "Oh yes, you mean my census name?"

"Under what name do you pay your taxes?" the policeman inquired.

"Oh . . . well, Mwenimuzi . . . No, Yotamu," the village headman was saying, frightened at the thought that the policemen's visit might be in connection with his tax, which he had not paid. "Yotamu Mwenimuzi, sir," he said, his hand still up.

"Simbwindimbwi here?" The policeman was reading his piece of paper.

"He just went behind the house, sir," the village headman said and dropped his hand sharply.

"Just a moment ago," Puccinni added.

"Do you live here too?" the policeman asked Puccinni.

"Me? Of course not," Puccinni said. "Why?"

The policeman ignored him and, turning his head to one of his subordinates, said, "Go fetch him from behind the house."

The policeman in question was the youngest-looking of the trio. He had a small face with large and apprehensive eyes and gave one the impression of being either lazy or very casual about his job. He nodded and walked slowly away, his baton swinging from his belt.

"Tepa . . . is he here?" the enormous policeman called.

"Yes, Bwana," Tepa answered from inside the house. "I am in here."

"Come out at once," the third policeman said in a harsh and commanding voice. "Come out and stand beside the others."

"Sinka?"

"I am right here," Sinka said in a rude and challenging voice as he appeared in the doorway, holding in his right hand a sweet potato, white with ashes.

"Come and stand here with the others," the policeman said. "I will ask you to throw away that potato."

Sinka held on to his potato, this time with both hands. He obviously meant to defy the policeman, but he threw it down when the village headman motioned to him to do as told. In the meantime the priest shrugged his shoulders as if to say "Hopeless," and sat down, crossing himself.

"There is nobody behind the house," the young-looking policeman who had gone to fetch Simbwindi-bwi reported. "There isn't a single person over there," he repeated.

"What do you mean, there is nobody over there?" the village headman asked.

"Well, there is nobody there."

The village headman himself went around the house twice and returned to give the same report.

"I am sorry," he said, "but you are right. There is really nobody there."

"Were you lying?" the enormous policeman asked brusquely. "You said he was there, but he isn't."

"I saw him, too," Puccinni said. "He was standing right here about a minute before you arrived . . ."

The two policemen spent some two hours looking for the missing doctor in every single house. They examined even the roofs, as though Simbwindimbwi might have turned himself into a bat or a rat, looked behind and under the pots, as though they were after something that was no bigger than a cockroach.

"He isn't anywhere," one of them told their leader.

"Did you look up in the trees?"

"In the trees?"

"He couldn't have disappeared so quickly," the leader said. "He must be hiding somewhere around here. Look in the barns, in the trees, everywhere . . ."

They did, but he was neither in the trees nor in the barns. He had disappeared.

"Moses," the leader said to the young-looking police-man, "I am afraid you will have to remain behind and see if you can catch this man Simbwindimbwi. We will send you a reinforcement tomorrow."

Moses blushed but remained silent and composed.

"Will all three of you," the leader instructed at the top of his voice, the emblem of his profession shining on the front of his cap, "please come with us to the Boma?"

"To the Boma? What for?" the village headman protested.

"Sir," the leader said with a grave and pretended politeness, the hair from his nostrils quivering as he spoke, "I can't command you, but the terms of the law demand that I ask you to jump into the car immediately."

"But my helmet, my robes, my . . ." the village headman was pleading.

Immediately the messenger came running out, carrying the helmet as well as a black pair of robes, followed shortly by the queen, who was heaving and speaking in a high-pitched soprano voice, "And where do you think you are taking him?"

The messenger delivered the items to the village headman, who jumped into the car with the other two men.

"You can stay," the leader told Musyani, who was about to jump into the car too. "We shall call for you if needed." Musyani, his shirt still gray with the dirt from the grave-digging the previous day, bowed lightly and retreated to join the priest, who was now standing beside his motorcycle under the tree.

The two policemen jumped into the front seats simultaneously, took off their caps and drove away, leaving Moses, who was standing with his hands thrust into his pockets. Musyani waved his hand and Puccinni stood beside his motorcycle, tears running down his face, waving.

"So long, friends!" he said.

Five days passed and Moses was still in the village waiting for his relief, as well as any news about the whereabouts of Simbwindimbwi. Puccinni, after distributing some candies to the children and stroking their cheeks, and throwing a pound note to the widow, which was accepted with both hands, had left for his Mission only a few hours after the Police. Simeon, his white bag over his shoulder, sandals on his feet, his trousers rolled up to his knees and his shirt unbuttoned, had gone to the next village, where he continued preaching and spreading the Word of Jehovah.

Moses stayed with Musyani and they became good friends, accompanying each other into the forests, where they spent the day setting up traps for pigs. Moses sat on rocks and hummed in low notes some military tunes.

Once, a fortuneteller revealed to Moses and Musyani that she knew Simbwindimbwi was hiding on the mountain. For a reasonable fee, she said, she could lead them to the exact spot of his hiding.

"Now, shall we make a deal?" the woman asked, her face beaming and the broad smile on her lips revealing a perfect set of yellow teeth.

"No deal," Moses said.

For the rest of the day Musyani tried and almost succeeded in persuading the policeman to listen to the woman whose power of fortunetelling he described as never failing.

"You want promotion?" he asked. "Believe me, you won't get it by sitting here like a woman. Listen to her. Go to the mountain like a man and capture him."

Moses shrugged his shoulders disinterestedly. He was tired, he said, and wished to rest. If the Boma was interested in Simbwindimbwi, they would have sent his reinforcement already.

"If you want to be promoted," Musyani told him, "you have to be a hero, and bless me if any man ever became a hero by doing nothing but sitting down and staring at the women's breasts day in and day out. Look at me," he continued, now speaking more excitedly, "I would be a general now if I had joined your profession."

"It's too bad that we don't have generals in the Police," Moses said with a sly smile on his face.

"Well, whatever they are called," Musyani said, "I would be one of them now. I would be a hero because I like to work."

"I am not going to be a hero," Moses said. "I don't want to be one."

In the meantime the village headman and his team were having entirely different experiences at the Boma.

"Don't tell me you are putting me in jail," the village headman had said after they had arrived at the Boma.

"Not really," the enormous policeman told him as he presented the three men to the prison attendant, with a note scribbled in pencil. "You can rest in there," he continued. "I am sure your honor is tired."

The tall, white-uniformed prison attendant with side whiskers and a rifle on his shoulder quickly escorted the newcomers into a relatively large and stinking cell.

"Hand me those articles," the attendant demanded.

"What? These?" the village headman retorted. "But they are mine."

"No personal articles are allowed here," the attendant said in a firm voice. "In a few moments I will have your clothes as well, since you are required to wear a uniform here. The government," he had continued with one corner of his mouth turned down, "will take very good care of you."

The cell had been dark when they entered and now that their eyes had accustomed themselves to the environment, the newcomers could see the dirty cement floor, with banana peels lying in one corner, the narrow windows high up on the walls, almost touching the ceiling, and eight tired men sitting down in single file, their backs against the brick wall, their heads shaved to the skull, all of them uniformed and looking much alike.

"Welcome home!" one of them said in a loud and sarcastic manner. "How long are you staying here, my good friends?"

"For the night, I should say," Sinka answered.

The eight men laughed.

"So they are turning this place into a hotel," another said. "Or are you in transit?"

"In transit?" the village headman asked. "What do you mean, in transit?"

"Well, what is your crime?" the same man asked.

"Crime?" the village headman said, his eyes widened in surprise and his hand extended toward the attendant, who was struggling with the bracelet, pulling it off for safekeeping. "We haven't committed any crime."

"What are you doing here, then?" one of the eight asked. "Do you know where you are?"

"At the Boma, of course," Sinka answered.

"In the Rest House?"

"No, in the prison."

"At least you know where you are," the same man said. "But I still can't understand why they would bring you here for no reason at all, or just for the night, as you say."

"Be quiet!" the attendant bellowed in his commanding voice.

The newcomers took off their clothes and stood still, avoiding each other's eyes, while the attendant brought them pairs of red overalls with two black stripes at the back and the front.

"Here," the attendant said, "put these on."

For five days the village headman and his team lived in the prison, wore prison uniforms, ate with the prisoners, but did not do any prison work. They stayed there and were referred to by the others as visitors or guests.

"Feed the visitors . . . wash their uniforms . . ." the others would complain to the attendant. "Why keep them here if they can't do anything."

Once a day the attendant would take them outside where they sat on the grass for hours while the prisoners were mowing lawns or burying bodies from the nearby hospital. Then he would escort them back to the cell and lock them up.

"How long would you say we are going to live here like this?" the village headman asked.

"I don't know," the attendant said. "I should say forever."

"Forever in this stinking place!" the village headman said and burst into stifled sobs. "My wife, poor woman!"

"He is crying!" one of the eight shouted. "We have wives too. We have children, but we aren't crying."

"Sit down and behave like a chief!" the attendant commanded. "If they lock you up here for the rest of your life, your wife will be permitted to visit you once in a while."

"Never believe a word from him," someone said. "He's just an attendant here and those matters are decided by those imprisoning you."

"One more word from you," the attendant said, "and I will cane you."

There was a sudden and forbidding silence as the prisoners and their three visitors, all looking alike in their red overalls, sat on the cement floor, their backs thrust again the wall, while the attendant was locking the door outside.

14

"He has not returned," Moses said as three policemen alighted from their vehicle one morning. "I don't think he is ever going to return to the village. Not soon, at any rate."

"Does anybody know where he might have gone?" a stern-looking policeman asked.

"There is an old woman who conjectures that he is on the mountain, hiding," Moses said, "but I don't think she knows what she is talking about."

"Where is she?"

"Somewhere in the village," Moses said. "Really, she is just guessing and she wants payment for her guess."

"Call her."

"I will if you are serious," Moses said and dispatched Musyani to collect the woman.

The queen, who had already declared herself ruler of the village in the absence of her husband, came tugging her weight and wagging her finger at the policemen.

"Tell me," she said, "where did you put him?"

"And who does she think she is?" the stern-looking policeman asked.

"She is the wife of the village headman," Moses said with great emphasis, "and she is sometimes quite unruly, so you better mind yourself when talking to her."

"You mean Mwenimuzi?" the stern one said with a flattering smile on his face. "He should be coming back as soon as we get hold of this Simbwindimbwi."

"You better bring him back!" the queen screeched.

In the meantime, the old soothsaying woman appeared, trotting behind Musyani and saying, "He didn't believe me. I know where Simbwindimbwi is."

"Where is he?" the stern one asked.

"There on the mountain," she said, pointing at the mountain.

"Are you sure he is up there?"

"I know he is up there."

"Come with us."

"But you have to pay me first," the woman said. "I am not going up there until you pay me."

"How much do you want?"

"How much do I want?" the old woman asked, her face aglow. "I would say ten shillings."

"You will get it when we catch him," the stern policeman said. "Come on, let's go."

"You can't order my people around like that," the queen said. "Pay her as she says, then you can order her."

"Pay me now, or I am not going anywhere," the old woman said and sneered at the policeman.

"Take her to the car," the stern-looking policeman said, and his two companions started advancing toward the old woman.

"Go back to your house," the queen told the old woman.

"Listen, woman," the policeman said, "if you want your husband back, you will have to cooperate with us."

"No stupid policeman is going to arrest my people," the queen said. "Go back to your house and we shall see how smart they think they are."

"To the car!"

"To your house!"

"Let her go," he said to his companions. "Let her go."

"I told you," Moses said, "you can't bully this woman."

"He's right," the queen said. "You aren't going to bully me. Pay her or go up to the mountain alone."

"Do you have ten shillings on you?" the stern-looking policeman asked one of his companions. "You will get a refund when we get back to the office."

"And what are we going to write in the books?" the other said. "Ten shillings for a fortuneteller!"

"Do you have ten shillings on you?" he repeated angrily. "Leave the details to me. All I want is ten shillings."

"No, I don't."

"I do," Musyani said. "I can lend it to you, but when do I get it back?"

"Give it to her," the policeman said. "You will get it back as soon as we get to the office, which may be today or tomorrow."

Musyani disappeared into his house and emerged shortly, holding in his hand an old and dirty ten shilling note, which he handed to the old woman, the latter now ululating with joy.

"Now," the stern policeman said, "are you ready? All four of us are going up with her," he continued, and Moses started complaining, saying that he thought they had come to relieve him.

"But you haven't been working all these days," the other said. "What are you complaining about?"

"Wait," the old woman said, a serious expression on her face. "Wait a moment."

"What is it you want now?" the policeman asked.

"Just wait," she said, the same expression still on her face. "Simbwindimbwi is very cunning. He knows that I know where he is hiding and that we are about to go up. I know what I will do."

Saying this, she ran to her house, leaving the policemen to wonder among themselves what on earth she was talking about. She came back a few minutes later.

"Here you are," she said, handing some roots to the policemen. "Put these in your pockets and they will lure him into sleep and he will not predict our coming."

They were already ascending the mountain, the four policemen, the old woman, and Musyani, who had brought along his spear and axe. The old woman, now more excited, was walking at the head of the group. The policemen, claiming that their boots were too heavy, were at the back and hardly able to keep pace with her.

"Hurry up," she called. "He's still there, asleep."

"I hope she knows what she is doing," one of the policemen said, wiping the sweat off his face with his shirt, "or I will knock her brains out."

"Hurry up!"

"Slow down," the policeman shouted. "Why are you in such a hurry?"

"You want to catch him, don't you?" she said, looking down at the policeman behind her. "Then hurry up!"

"You can trust her," Musyani said. "If she says he's there, he is there."

"We shall see sooner or later," the stern-looking policeman said.

The policemen took off their shirts and carried them

over their shoulders as they walked up the mountain in single file.

"Do you see him?" one of the policemen asked.

"Certainly," the woman answered.

"He is asleep?"

"He is asleep," she agreed with him. "He is sitting down, leaning against a stump."

By noon they were already at the top. Then they followed her down an embankment into a running stream, where after washing their faces, the policemen amused themselves by throwing rocks at butterflies and bees flying around the flowers.

"Follow me," she said. "We are almost there, and be quiet."

"Is she serious?" one of the policemen said.

"You can trust her," Musyani said.

"Shhhh!" went the old woman, a finger on her lips. "He's behind that tree," she said in a whisper.

They tiptoed to the place, pieces of wood cracking under the policemen's boots. The policemen thought the whole thing both stupid and amusing.

When they had come within four feet of the place the woman, pointing at a stump on the farther end, said in a whisper, "There he is, do you see him?"

The stern-looking policeman thrust his head over the woman's shoulder and he could see a pair of legs, long and rugged, and then the head leaning against a stump.

"He's still asleep," the woman whispered.

"I don't believe it!" the stern-looking policeman said in a loud voice. "Tell me, am I seeing things?"

The woman was about to place her hand over the policeman's mouth to keep it shut when Simbwindim- bwi rose and rubbed his eyes. He looked at the six people and smiled, made a motion with his legs as if about to advance toward them, but when he realized what it was all about, the smile vanished and he took off at a terrific speed, branches falling off the trees behind him.

"He's fled!" Musyani said. "Let's run after him."

"Stupid me!" the stern-looking policeman said. "I should have kept my mouth shut."

"There he goes," the woman said.

"Can we catch up with him now?" the same policeman asked.

"Catch up with Simbwindimbwi?" the woman gasped. "He runs like a deer, that one. Now that he is frightened, he will run all day and probably all night. It will be forty or fifty miles before he decides to stop and rest."

They were now standing at the place where he had been lying.

"He has been feeding on potatoes," one of the policemen said, kicking his boots into a pile of decaying sweet potatoes. "I wonder where he got them."

A wet blanket was hanging on a branch, and his cowbells and some roots were sitting under the stump and next to a dying fire.

"This is all the property the poor man has," Moses said.

"You have earned your money, dear woman," the stern-looking policeman said, "but I still can't understand it. You would," he added thoughtfully, "be very useful in the Police Force."

"I would?" the woman said with a wide grin on her face.

They walked back to the village, tired and silent all the way down. Once in the village, the policemen, all four of them, thanked the woman and jumped into the car, promising they would send Musyani his money the following day.

15

A short, plump policeman, his uniform neatly pressed, was blowing the morning bugle under the flagpole at the Boma. People would soon start hurrying to their offices and shops. Prisoners would be escorted from their cells to the outside world, teeming with fresh air, where they would toil all day long.

The Boma itself is situated on the lakeshore. On a happy and clear morning like this, one sees scores of canoes far out on the lake as fishermen come home to sleep. Children run to the lake to play on the sand for the rest of the day and women in multicolored dresses, pots balanced on their heads, sing their way to the lake to draw water. If there is no work for the prisoners, they are ordered to the lake to scoop sand into huge buckets and carry it to the Boma. They do this all day long. If there is no work for them tomorrow, they will be ordered to return the sand to the lake.

The policeman under the flagpole blew his bugle, minding his notes with the same care he would if he were performing in a concert hall. The attendant unlocked the door and let his prisoners out while another guard, armed, stood stiffly nearby. The four policemen who had returned from the village the previous evening and who had already submitted their reports to their superiors, walked by on their way to the office. Shortly, the enormous policeman and his white master appeared, both dressed in uniforms.

"Will Yotamu Mwenimuzi and his group please follow us to the office?" the enormous policeman announced to the guard. "Bring them along immediately."

"Yes, sir," the guard said, saluting the white officer.

The white man paced the floor of his office, his hands in his pockets. The enormous policeman stood at the other end of the desk, a bunch of papers in his hand. The village headman and Sinka and Tepa sat on the bench parallel to the whitewashed wall, with the armed guard standing at attention near the door.

"They weren't able to catch Simbwindimbwi," the enormous policeman said, "but it will be a matter of time before he is caught."

"Yotamu Mwenimuzi," the white man called, still pacing the floor, "you allowed a dangerous man namely Simbwindimbwi, to live in your village."

"Yes, Bwana," the village headman said.

"You knew for quite some time that Sinka believed that Musyani had bewitched Matenda and that he was going to kill him."

"Yes, Bwana."

"And you did not take any action against him," the white man said, sitting down in an armchair behind his desk.

"No, Bwana."

At the command of the armed guard, the three men rose to their feet, because the white man was now sitting down.

"I have a report here that you kept mwavi in your house," the white man continued. "Is that true?"

"Yes, Bwana."

"Do you know that it is against the law of this land?"

"Yes, Bwana."

"Sinka and Tepa," the white man called, "a few nights ago you burned the house of one Musyani with intent to kill, did you not?"

"Yes, Bwana."

"But you denied that to me!" the village headman said.

"Be quiet," the guard said.

The white man rose and resumed his pacing, while the guard motioned the three men to sit down.

"Yotamu Mwenimuzi, do you still keep mwavi in your house?" he asked.

"Yes, Bwana."

"Will you let us have it?"

"Yes, Bwana."

"All right," he said, resuming his seat. The others rose to their feet.

There was a general silence that lasted for about five minutes while the white man, his hands folded and lying on the desk, gazed at the wall before him in a meditative mood. Then he rose again, and the others sat down.

"Do you know that you all have committed crimes?" he asked in a stern voice.

"Yes, Bwana," all three said together.

"In the absence of the District Commissioner," he began, "and in exercise of the powers invested in me, I charge you, Yotamu Mwenimuzi, with negligence in the exercise of your duties, and I am sending you to prison for a period of one year.

"I charge you, Sinka and Tepa, with willfully burning Musyani's house with intent to destroy life, and I am sentencing you to hard labor for a period of six years. Dismissed."

The three prisoners, now weeping, were escorted back to the cell to start their terms. A lookout notice was sent for Simbwindimbwi, who was now placed on the list of wanted men.